Like a lot of people, Ben Adams college, and eventually grew up a job, a house and a family.

And then his mid-life crisis kicked in…

Realising that life was in danger of becoming all too serious, Ben started writing. Not in the way that Forrest Gump started running, but at least he started.

He wrote on steamed up mirrors in the bathroom to make his children smile. Eventually he graduated to making up stories to entertain his kids at bed-time.

For some reason, his boys didn't seem interested in his tales of everyday life, relationships, family, trauma, farce and the occasional bit of debauchery. His sons told him they preferred JK someone or other.

Following his short-lived career as a children's author, Ben now concentrates on writing stories for grown-ups. He writes for people who have lived, loved, worked, strived and suffered – people like him. People like you.

Ben lives in southwest London with his two boys and his dog.

To receive information on Ben's next book, visit www.benadamsauthor.com to sign-up to Ben's mailing list, and follow Ben on Twitter @benadamsauthor.

Praise for Ben Adams' Debut Novel:
Six Months to Get a Life

'Adams throws in comedic timing to perfection.'
– Chick Lit Central

'A fun, entertaining and realistic story…'
– A Spoonful of Happy Endings

'A well-written, enjoyable, contemporary
drama of life after divorce…'
– Eat, Sleep, Read, Review

SIX LIES

BEN ADAMS

SilverWood

Published in 2015 by SilverWood Books

SilverWood Books Ltd
14 Small Street, Bristol, BS1 1DE, United Kingdom
www.silverwoodbooks.co.uk

ISBN 978-1-78132-455-4 (paperback)
ISBN 978-1-78132-456-1 (ebook)

British Library Cataloguing in Publication Data
A CIP catalogue record for this book is available from
the British Library

Set in Sabon by SilverWood Books
Printed on responsibly sourced paper

For my latest internet date. You're lovely x

Dear David

Dear David,
As your dad is fond of saying, rectal cancer is a pain in the backside.

If you're reading this letter then the wretched disease has got the better of me. As I scribble away in my bedroom, I know my time is running out. I have fought my heart out over the past couple of years to fend off my cancer, but life has become too painful. I'm running out of energy. Once I've finished this letter, I plan to accept any drugs on offer and drift off quietly into oblivion. My time has come.

Over the past few days, I've been dwelling on what difference I've made to the world. This may sound a bit clichéd but, believe me, when you know you'll be dying soon, the urge to look back rather than think about a future you won't be part of is irresistible.

I've never wanted fame and fortune. I won't be studied by generations of school children or idolised by thousands of sports fans. I don't suppose even the music world will mourn my passing despite my accomplishments with a sax over the years.

None of that matters to me though. When I look

back on my life, I feel contented. I have been to great places, met great people and had great times. I've done alright.

Without a doubt, your dad's and my greatest contribution to this world is you.

You might still have some rough edges (you get them from your father) but when you aren't being grumpy, you're a joy to be around and a positive influence on everyone you meet. When you walk into a room, people smile. Your enthusiasm for life is infectious. Everyone you meet falls for your charms.

You didn't achieve your dream of being the next Billy Joel or Liverpool's record striker, but even if you had done, your father and I wouldn't have been more proud of you than we already are. We love you more than you could ever know and I for one will go to my grave in the knowledge that I've brought up a unique, sparky and fun-loving son.

I'm truly sorry to be leaving you. It hurts that I'll never again get to share a pot of tea with you on your way home from work. I won't get to play cards with you and your dad, or discover new restaurants with the pair of you. I won't get to hear about all those scrapes you get yourself into on a regular basis. I won't get to meet your next 'chosen one'. On that subject, rather than just choosing a new woman each night, don't you think it's about time you chose someone to settle down with? And if it's still Louise you want, then bloody well do something about it.

Even if it is only to tell you how proud I am of you, this letter would be worth writing. Unfortunately, that isn't its sole purpose. There's something else I need to say.

Whatever way I put this, it will shock you, so I will just come out with it. Biologically speaking, I'm not your mother.

Those words must be truly shocking to you. I can imagine your sharp intake of breath. You're probably swearing. You've certainly got every right to.

Your father can tell you the full story. Both of us have our own reasons for not telling you the truth sooner. Dad can explain himself, but let me tell you why I didn't open up to you. It came down to selfishness really. I didn't want you ever doubting my love for you. No one could have loved you more than me. You weren't my flesh and blood, but that made absolutely no difference to me.

I don't know what else to say now. Do you remember you used to come home from school every Wednesday and tell me how many goals you had scored in your school football game? And then one Wednesday you came home hot and agitated, shouting, "Mum, Mum, I really scored a goal today!"

I love you, son.

Mum

Part One

Dave Fazackerley

Chapter One

'If anyone's sober at the end of my wake, I'll come back from the dead and kick your arse.'

Mum's last words to me before she died were going through my head as I did up my gaudy red tie on the morning of her funeral. She was that sort of character, the life and soul, the heartbeat of our family. Things were never dull with Mum around. And she hadn't wanted the last party in her honour to be dull either.

As these occasions tend to be, her funeral started off fairly sedately. The service was held at St Martin's, the church Mum used to worship at, if you call singing carols on Christmas Eve worshipping. The service was fairly standard. The vicar did a good job, although he did struggle to pronounce Mum's name. To be fair, Valerie Juniper Fazackerley isn't the easiest name in the world to enunciate. Most people just called her Mrs F, which was what Dad eventually advised the holy man to do.

Mum was then buried at the attractively named Merton and Sutton Joint Cemetery. Dad will join her there at some point, but hopefully not any time soon.

The turnout at her send-off would have pleased Mum. The requisite amount of close family and friends were there, suited and booted, most in black despite Dad having issued instructions to the contrary. A bunch of 1970s hippy musos turned up too. They added a bit more colour to proceedings, both in their dress and in their language. 'What the fuck am I doing up at this time in the morning,' John the bass player grumbled as he shook my hand outside the church. The musicians' role was to play a passable version of Norman Greenbaum's 'Spirit in the Sky' at the wake, a song many of the same faces had played at Mum and Dad's wedding nearly forty-five years previously.

We held the wake in the Morden Brook, the pub across the roundabout from the cemetery. The bar staff were great with our party, laying on free sandwiches and giving us our own room to be miserable in. They needn't have bothered. At Mum's instruction, we were less miserable than the pub's regulars.

Mum was sent on her way with as much nostalgic storytelling and laughter as we could muster. There was our old neighbour, Gary, regaling us with tales of their shared youth. 'Your mother was a right goer in her time, son. The stories I could tell you…' No thanks, Gary.

Or there was Anna from the flower shop, an old school friend of Mum's. 'She always had her choice of the boys, did your mum. She was the first one of us to get boobs. We were so jealous.' Thanks for that, Anna.

And there was Dad. 'I'm going to miss the old bird. I'll have to make my own hot chocolate when I go to bed tonight.' His feelings obviously ran deep.

'You did her proud, son,' people who I had never met kept telling me as they scoffed another free sandwich. Half of them had probably never met Mum either.

Even Louise, my wife who ran off with a librarian, popped in to pay her respects.

Lou and Mum had been close when the two of us were a couple. They used to enjoy a Saturday afternoon routine of visiting nail and eye bars together, and often the odd wine bar too. Mum told me once that my wedding day was the happiest day of her life. Dad wasn't impressed with that reflection. 'What about ours?' he asked, with a mock hurt expression on his face. Or maybe it wasn't mock.

'That wasn't bad, either,' Mum admitted, 'until you collapsed on the bed and fell asleep with your tux on.'

'I never did.'

'You did. I had to get your lecherous best man to unzip my wedding dress for me, otherwise I'd have been forced to sleep in it all night. Some start to my honeymoon that was.'

'Your Mum was one of the kindest people I've ever known,' Lou told me while doing her best not to drop crumbs from some nondescript funeral food over the pub carpet.

But then Lou had run off with the librarian and Mum had stopped getting her nails done. 'I thought the last time you saw her, she had called you a tart and cancelled her library membership,' I commented.

'That aside, she was one of the kindest people I've ever known. And besides, that wasn't the last time I saw her.'

'It wasn't?'

'No, I saw her quite a few times when she was ill.'

That was a surprising development, and one that ever so slightly irked me. Although Lou had run off with the librarian (have I mentioned that once or twice already?), we hadn't got divorced. Technically speaking at least, she was still my wife. Shouldn't Mum have told me she had started meeting up with my wife again?

As per Mum's instructions, her wake was a drunken affair. By the end of the night, the stories of her antics were getting more outrageous. Unfortunately, or maybe fortunately, my memory of the details got hazier as the alcohol dulled my brain. When the lights were dimmed and we were turfed out of the pub, Mum would have been relaxing in the knowledge that she didn't have to put in an appearance from beyond the grave to propel her boot into my backside.

The day after Mum's funeral was never going to be a barrel of laughs, but I would rather not have started it off feeling like I was barely in the land of the living myself. My head was about to explode and my stomach felt as though it was devouring itself from within. When I eventually crawled out of bed, the morning was nearly over. Coffee and pills were the order of the day.

Getting into my boxers and negotiating the stairs tested my co-ordination to its limits. Fortunately, there was nowhere pressing for me to be that day. My employers, a well-known multi-national bank, had kindly given me a few days off work. 'Compassionate leave', they called it. They weren't really being compassionate though, they just didn't want me being miserable in front of their customers.

As I sat at my breakfast bar nursing my coffee, I began to realise how hard it was going to be to get used to Mum not being around anymore. Her passing had created a void in my life, a void that, at that moment, I doubted I would ever completely fill.

The clink of the letter box disturbed my reverie. Looking up, I saw the postwoman retreating down the drive. She turned and smiled at me. Lip-reading isn't one of my specialities but I swear she mouthed 'nice legs' before turning the corner. Lou and I never got around to buying net curtains.

Feeling slightly embarrassed, I got up to see what news she had delivered. There were quite a few 'commiserations on your loss' cards. As I sifted through them with little enthusiasm, one envelope stopped me in my tracks.

Ever since I was a boy, Mum's handwriting had captivated me. It was artsy, enthusiastic, full of flourishes and embellishments. If anyone showed their personality through their scrawl, Mum did. Creative and slightly quirky. The envelope that caught my attention had been addressed by Mum.

Tossing the other cards on the kitchen counter, I prised Mum's letter open and laid the two pages of expensive note paper out in front of me. My chest felt tight, my hangover temporarily forgotten as I read Mum's words.

Her communication from the grave was like a bonus life in a computer game. Just when I thought she had gone, I got to spend a bit more time with her.

Reading about Mum's pride in me brought tears to my eyes. She had been fairly free with her praise when it was warranted, so her pride didn't come as a surprise. She had also been prepared to speak her mind and give me a good dressing down if she thought I deserved one. So reading her dig about it being time I found someone to settle down with made me smile. I had heard it many times before.

But of course neither her pride in me nor her desire for me to settle down would have made the headlines in the story of my life. Those comments would only have appeared as a small article on page six, next to an account of my mate Graham's treacherous thieving of my packed lunch during some boring school geography trip in the early 80s.

The headlines in the story of my life would, at that moment, have been dominated by Mum's bombshell. 'Biologically speaking, I'm not your mother.'

When I got to that part in her letter, I stared open-mouthed at the words in front of me. Hot coffee dribbled down my chin until I remembered to swallow. And breathe. Putting my coffee down, I rubbed my eyes. When my gaze returned to the letter, the words were still there. I hadn't imagined them. *What the hell?*

The letter was much thumbed by the end of the morning. I have read it a thousand times since, too. My immediate reaction was one of complete shock. Mum's revelation was incomprehensible. I couldn't even begin to understand its significance, let alone think about what to do next. If Mum wasn't my mother, then a huge chunk of my life had been a lie.

How could she not be my mother? After all, there were photos of Mum holding me as a baby on practically every surface and wall of my parents' house. Too many photos, in my humble opinion.

Feeling overwhelmed, I returned Mum's letter to its envelope and stumbled back to bed.

Chapter Two

Surprisingly, Mum's revelation wasn't at the forefront of my mind in the first few days after her funeral. I pretty much wrote the matter off as the ramblings of a mad woman dosed up on painkillers. As far as I knew, there had never been any scandal in our household. Mum and Dad had been together since the Beatles...since the Stones...since, well, always. She must have lost her marbles during those last few painful days of her life.

The insanity argument didn't totally grip me, but it was a convenient line to take when all I wanted to do was wallow in my grief and remember the good times with Mum.

It was impossible to forget her at first. When I went shopping, I would see food she liked eating. When I listened to music, Mum's favourites would invariably bring memories flooding back. I even thought of Mum when I was putting my shirts on the line. She had this odd way of hanging them upside down using three pegs.

Until her cancer dragged her down, Mum was more energetic than people half her age. She would regularly dance the night away at a party and still be up at the crack of dawn to take on a new challenge.

Her holidays were legendary too. 'Why the hell would I want to climb a mountain in Borneo,' Dad grumbled a couple of years ago when Mum told him about their next adventure.

Rather than letting life shape her, Mum had shaped life. She always knew what she wanted and, more often than not, she would find a way of getting it. She had done her best to instil the same ethos in me when I was growing up.

When I wasn't selected to play in the school band and came home moaning about it, Mum made me write down ten things I could do to change the music teacher's decision. My list, which included frivolous entries such as 'superglue Andrew's fingers to his synthesiser' and 'bribe Mr Heath', had been pinned to my parents' fridge for years.

Mum persuaded me to pursue the entry that had simply read 'play more, play louder'. With Mum's encouragement, I went into school the next morning and played the school's grand piano as the five hundred or so students shuffled in to the hall for assembly. Despite punishing me for my 'flagrant disregard of school protocol', Mr Heath eventually relented and gave me a place in the band.

One of the things I admired most about Mum was her spirit. She didn't sit back, waiting for life to do her any favours. She got off her backside and pursued her dreams. Judging by her comments in her letter to me, she had been pretty happy with her lot when she died. Was I happy with my lot? Was I pursuing my dreams?

As a rule, introspection doesn't come naturally to the males in the Fazackerley household. Self-doubt is not something Dad or I experience too often. In the period after Lou ran off with the librarian, I banned introspection altogether, preferring instead to take the far less painful route of going down the pub and getting drunk to fill my time. But, on a wet Saturday evening a few days after Mum's funeral, as I ironed my shirts in preparation for my imminent return to work, I caught myself beginning to think about my own lot. Maybe I had spent too long on my own that week.

I had certainly been living the dream when I was with Lou. In my mind at least, we were the perfect couple. We first met on Graham's stag night. Stag nights in those days weren't spent in Blackpool, Dublin or Las Vegas. People only tended to go on a local pub crawl. As Graham's best man, I had organised a tour of the local hostelries in Putney.

About ten of us started off in the Prince of Wales, moved on to the Fox and Hounds, and then gradually worked our way down the high street towards Coasts by Putney Bridge. By the time we reached the club, we were well oiled but not too far gone to enjoy the delights of the obligatory strippergram.

The stripper was booked for eleven. At eleven on the dot, a gorgeous girl in a long fur coat parted the sea of dancers like she had taken lessons from Moses and made her way towards our group. The fur coat reached down to her bare knees. I could only imagine what she was wearing underneath it. And boy, did I imagine.

As the Best Man and designated group leader for the night, I introduced myself.

'Hi, Dave. Nice to meet you,' she replied in a classy-sounding Home Counties accent.

We looked at each other for a few awkward

seconds before I asked her how this was meant to work. Inexplicably, David Rose's classic trombone jazz beat hadn't kicked in. 'You are meant to ask me my name, I think.'

'Er, Patricia? Crystal?'

'Louise.'

'Louise, right.' She was stunning. Beginning to salivate, I tried to move things on a pace. 'So, do you dance or what?'

'I can do.'

'And then what?'

She had raised her eyebrows at that one. 'Well, that depends, doesn't it?'

'Fucking hell, this is hard work,' I grumbled, 'I didn't realise you had to chat up a stripper to get her to do her job these days.'

The slap in the face I received from my future wife left me with a red cheek for the rest of the night.

The actual stripper, who turned up as I was holding the ice from my whisky glass against my cheek, wasn't in the same league as Lou. In fact, whereas Lou was in peak physical condition, the stripper was definitely in the veterans' league. She was old enough to be my mother and large enough that contour lines appeared on a map wherever she went.

As the trombones began to play, 'voluptuous Vera' began to remove her attire. Bits wobbled that shouldn't have wobbled, and other parts drooped that shouldn't have drooped. Certainly amongst our party anyway. It may sound a little cruel, but anyone who had eaten before coming out for the evening was in severe danger of being reacquainted with their dinner.

The Graham Hope stag party was the laughing stock of the club. Even Lou joined in with the piss-taking. 'How could you mistake me for that strippergran,' she asked once I had apologised to her for the umpteenth time.

Things developed swiftly between Lou and me from there, to the extent that Lou was my 'plus one' at Graham's wedding the following Saturday.

Lou made me feel alive when I was with her in a way that no one else ever has. When we were together, we would share everything, talk about anything and always find something to laugh about. Life was never boring for me with Lou.

She is gorgeous too. She used to be a lingerie model for Ann Summers. Now, she's a marketing executive, whatever that means.

The two of us tied the knot within a year of me calling her a stripper. We were the proverbial perfect couple.

And then one day she decided I wasn't going anywhere in my career. She wanted ambition. Then my lack of ambition became lack of intelligence. My mates saw a certain irony in a blonde, former lingerie model telling me I wasn't intelligent enough for her.

And finally, about two years ago, Lou upped and left to go and live with the librarian. I work in a bank. When I pointed out the inconsistency of her moaning at my lack of ambition and then shacking up with a man who stacked books for a living, Lou told me where to go. 'Oh, and I'll have you know, he's a manager, not a librarian,' she added. In my book, no pun intended, if he works in a library then he's a dork. I mean librarian.

Lou left me to rattle about on my own in our modern three-bedroom marital home. There were definitely some plusses to having the house to myself. My evenings were undoubtedly better for not having to watch endless period dramas. Lou was obsessed with the bloody programmes.

When Lou ditched me, I pretty much threw myself straight back into my previous happy-go-lucky single life. Nights in were to be avoided at all costs as they increased the likelihood that introspection, that nasty beast, would embed its talons into my forehead and twist and scratch until I screamed.

I met some fun women, discovered some good pubs and restaurants and kept the fishing tackle in working order. My womanising antics kept me busy and my mojo gradually began to recover from the near-fatal wounds inflicted on it by my wife and the librarian. On the surface at least, I was doing OK.

Mum wasn't convinced though. She wasn't impressed by my antics. On my first wedding anniversary after Lou had moved out, Mum invited me round for Lancashire hotpot. Having nothing better to do that evening, and not wishing to spend my time dwelling on what Lou was doing on our anniversary, I willingly accepted Mum's invitation.

As I clutched my knife and fork, Mum started in on me.

'It's been a while now, David, hasn't it?'

'What's been a while, Mum?'

'Since Lou left you.'

'Thanks for reminding me. It's been a few months, yes,' I admitted.

'And how are you coping?'

'Fine, thanks. This mutton's nice.' Analysing my lifestyle wasn't my favourite pastime.

Mum wasn't to be distracted from her chosen topic, though. She directed her fire at my 'string' of fairly short-term partners. 'I can see why you haven't introduced me to any of them. They sound like your personal branch of Alcoholics Anonymous.' Calling it a 'string' may well have been more misleading than the AA reference.

'If you want to settle down and have children, then you need to stop messing about,' she added, continuing her onslaught.

'Who says I want to settle down and have children?' I voiced my intention never to settle down again but Mum wouldn't be put off by what she saw as my defeatist attitude.

'Where are you going with your life at the moment?'

'I don't know, do I always have to be going somewhere?'

Other stock phrases Mum called upon that evening included, 'You're no spring chicken now, you know', and, 'Stop behaving like a twat'. OK, she said student, but I got the message.

It was only after her death, as I ironed my shirts on that wet October night, that I really thought about Mum's words. The fact is, she was right. Being single had become depressing. The thrill of the chase wasn't what it once was. Even the sex wasn't that satisfying after a while. Casual sex is better than no sex at all, but it's meaningless when compared with intimacy with someone you love.

Putting the sex to one side, what I really missed

was being able to share my highs and lows with that 'someone special'. What I needed that week in particular was someone who would willingly listen to my reminiscing about Mum. Someone who would put their own worries on hold just to help me unburden myself. Someone who cared. What I needed in the longer term was someone I could laugh at that inane programme on the telly with, someone I could cook for, someone I could travel the world with, one Greek island at a time. People talk about a problem shared being a problem halved, but it's also true that a joy shared is a joy doubled. Or a laugh shared is a lot bloody funnier. If all I had to look forward to in life was a succession of conquests, then I wouldn't be growing old happy.

As I hung my last shirt back in my wardrobe, the ironing done for the next week or so, I concluded that as well as missing Mum, I was missing Lou. Lou would always find the right words to say to make the world feel warm and exciting. I was never miserable when I was with Lou.

Mum had seen through my bluster. Without me ever having to admit it to her, she knew I wanted to settle down again. And she also seemed to know that I wanted Lou back. No one else would do.

Lou was my best mate, my better half, the brain that complemented my brawn, my sense of humour and the best shag I have ever had. We were meant to be together.

Knowing your life is drifting is one thing, but doing something about it is another. That's the bit that Mum was good at. She didn't tolerate drifting. Had she still been around, she would have pinned me down to a plan of action.

So, after my introspection, I made a vow to myself. No more messing about. I was going to win Lou back and no wimpy librarian book dork was going to stand in my way.

Admittedly, there were a few empty pint glasses on the table at the Raynes Park Tavern by the time this vow was made. Graham had phoned as I was putting the ironing board away, instructing me to get what he eloquently termed as my 'miserable arse' down the pub.

Graham was big on setting life goals. He had set himself a whole series of objectives on the day his divorce came through. He hadn't done too badly in achieving those goals either, although I would never tell him that.

I told Graham about my desire to get back with Lou. That discussion was relatively serious. Graham only threw a few 'you sad git's and 'get a life's in. But when I moved the conversation on to Mum's revelation, instead of giving me a sympathetic ear, Graham must have used up his quota of seriousness for the night because he took the conversation in an entirely different direction.

'So if Mrs F wasn't your mother, who the hell is, then?'

'I'm buggered if I know.'

'Maybe your parents stole you from some poor unsuspecting young couple?'

'Yeah, right.'

'What about that fat cow in the corner there drinking the triple vodka and dribbling down her chins? Your dad could have shagged her.'

'Maybe Dad shagged *your* mother. We might be

brothers,' I retorted, stooping to Graham's level or even lower. The pint glasses had been replaced by whisky tumblers by this point in the conversation, hence the deteriorating standards.

Graham's final theory before I cut him off was that Dad had indulged Maggie Thatcher. Graham always had me down as a bit of a Tory boy on account of me working in a bank.

When I didn't respond, Graham sat back in his chair and at last managed to wipe the grin off his face, replacing it with a thoughtful look. 'Presumably you're going to talk to your dad about all this?'

Even before that night's drinking, I had been finding it increasingly difficult to banish Mum's revelation from my mind. Despite trying to convince myself otherwise, I knew she hadn't lost her marbles. The clarity of her letter didn't suggest a befuddled mind.

Her parting shot must have been true, but that didn't necessarily mean I wanted to know the whole truth. The secret my parents kept from me until the day Mum died could taint my memory of Mum forever. Even knowing there was a secret pissed me off.

'I don't care what secret my parents kept from me,' I tried convincing Graham. 'Mum was Mum. She was the woman I respected, loved, confided in, took for granted and sponged off, from when I was a kid right up to the day she died. That's good enough for me.'

'That's all true, but it's bollocks too,' Graham argued. 'You're deluding yourself if you think you can just dismiss something like this out of hand.'

In my heart I knew my friend was right. Even

before Graham started speculating about my parentage, I had caught myself spending an increasing amount of time wondering about my back story. Did Dad get up to no good? Was I adopted? If so, why did my real mother give me up?

'What must it have been like for Mum to carry such a big secret around for so long?' I asked when Graham returned with yet another round of drinks. 'I can't keep a secret for five minutes, let alone forty years.'

'I know, you arse. Remember when I told you Helen was pregnant? You couldn't even keep your trap shut about that, could you?' Graham was right, somehow I had managed to spill the beans to his sister, Hilary. Hilary told Graham's mum, thereby robbing him of that pleasure.

We were the last to leave the pub that night. As I wended, or more accurately swayed, weaved and bumped my way home, I knew Graham was right. I needed to find out Mum and Dad's secret.

So I added 'find my birth mother' to 'win Lou back' on my mental list of life goals.

Chapter Three

Music is a big part of my life. In the days after Mum's death, I did a fair bit of what I tend to do when everything isn't hunky dory – shut myself away in my garage and play with my keyboard.

I come from musical stock. Or at least I thought I did prior to reading Mum's letter. My imposter mum, who I still thought of as Mum, was a saxophonist. She spent her youth and much of her early adult life playing in various jazz bands around Europe.

Dad was a session guitarist. He shared a recording studio and occasionally a stage with some pretty decent bands in the late 60s and early 70s. He even claims to have appeared on *Top of the Pops* a couple of times.

There was always music playing somewhere in my parents' house when I was young. The soundtrack to my childhood years was an eclectic mix of jazz and mainstream pop. Dad originally heralded from Liverpool, so The Beatles and The Hollies featured heavily during my formative years. Later, Pink Floyd, ELO, Supertramp, Human League and of course Squeeze were a major influence on me. Squeeze was without doubt my favourite band. I took up keyboards rather than the guitar, much to Dad's disgust.

I have been in a variety of groups over the years, none of which have ever made it big. To be honest, none have made it small either. My current outfit, Life in the Faz Lane, was, at the time of Mum's death, based in the garage of my house on Rectory Close in Raynes Park.

Life in the Faz Lane is a half-decent band. Actually we are a third-decent band. I'm pretty good but the other two are bordering on useless – and the wrong side of the border at that. As the keyboard player, I am the Jools Holland of the band. I am lead vocalist too, but only because I've heard the other two sing.

Jeremy Monk is our drummer. I've known Jeremy since we were teenagers. He lives two doors down from my parents. His family bought the house in the mid-eighties. They hadn't lived there long when either Jeremy heard me playing my synthesiser or I heard him beating the shit out of his drums. We struck up a music-based friendship, if not necessarily a life friendship. He is a drummer, after all.

Jeremy still lives in his parents' house, but his parents, who were both eminent bankers back in the day, have long since migrated southwards, to somewhere warm and no doubt less taxing.

In most ways, Jeremy is your typical drummer. When he isn't wielding his drumsticks, he is usually hefting a bottle of Jack Daniels with equal vigour. With his long hair and tattooed arms, he looks the part too. But Jeremy also happens to have followed in his parents' footsteps. By night he is a drummer, but by day he wears long-sleeved shirts to cover up the tattoos. He is my boss at the bank. Yes, the drummer in our band is a bank manager. Be worried. Be very worried.

And then there's Jason Wood, my cousin and our guitar maestro. Robin, Mum's brother and Jason's dad, used to be something big in the army. His family travelled a fair bit when we were younger. When they were in the UK, they spent a lot of time with the Fazackerley household. Whereas I preferred the keyboards, guitar-playing Dad found a willing pupil in Jason. He still isn't a patch on Dad, but Jason has turned into a passable strummer.

In a vague and ultimately hopeless attempt to seem more rock n' roll, Jeremy and Jason have, over the years, become Jezz and Jay. Jeremy is happy to be Jezz away from work but he banned me from using his nickname in front of work colleagues – a rule I assiduously follow.

There used to be four of us in the band. 'Boring Bren' used to play the bass. We went to school with Boring Bren. He was OK, but lacked a few social skills. Like talking and listening. And then there was his dubious taste in music. I could cope with Jezz being obsessed with Phil Collins and tapping out the beat from 'In the Air Tonight' incessantly during practices. I could even cope with Jay's Brian May impressions. But having a bass guitarist with an obsession for Whitney Houston was just too weird. Bren left Life in the Faz Lane due to irreconcilable musical differences.

We didn't rehearse much in the couple of months leading up to Mum's death, but a week or so after the funeral, I called the band to order. Life goes on.

As a band, we used to rehearse regularly. None

of us was sure what we were rehearsing for, but we rehearsed nonetheless, presumably in the hope that, one day, a gig would come along. Our last gig, and our biggest to date, took place about a year ago. We played at the Half Moon in Putney. The Half Moon booked us because I was having a thing with the barmaid and one of their acts had let them down at short notice. Obviously we didn't dwell on those facts when we told our mates we were following in the footsteps of real rock legends.

Our repertoire was pretty limited. In keeping with our suburban Raynes Park surroundings, we played bland, middle of the road, inoffensive stuff. Like Raynes Park, we were behind the curve when it came to being cool.

In our first practice since Mum died, without much effort, we nailed pretty passable versions of Soft Cell's 'Tainted Love' and Bowie's 'Let's Dance'. Our cover of 'Hungry Like the Wolf' wasn't too shabby either. But a combination of Jezz's propensity to consume at least one finger of Jack Daniels between each beat and my emotional instability meant that we completely ruined 'Part-time Lover' and 'I Need You Tonight'.

Once we had given up on the music for the night and retired to the Raynes Park Tavern, Jay came up with a fairly off-the-wall suggestion of a way to give our practices some focus. 'Why don't we just show up somewhere and start playing?' he suggested.

'What, like buskers?' I asked.

'Yes, only better.' Jay obviously had a low opinion of buskers.

After a few beers, this suggestion seemed to take

on a life of its own. It would be nice to play in front of a live audience. We agreed to do it a week later, on a Sunday afternoon. But where could we play?

Various options were suggested. We ruled out the circular bit of expensive-looking pavement outside Wimbledon station on the grounds that there were bound to be police in Wimbledon town centre who would send us on our way before we had even warmed up. The paved area outside the ugly monstrosity that serves as the council offices in Morden was ruled out on account of it being a shit hole. We finally settled on pitching up outside Raynes Park station between the coffee shop and the estate agent. The deciding factor was that we could always pop into the Tavern for a pint if things didn't go well.

We argued about song orders for our impromptu performance until closing time.

The following day was my first day back at work since Mum's death. As I rubbed my swollen eyes, I regretted ordering that last round of Scotches in the RPT.

I work in the City. That catch-all phrase is the one I use when I am trying to impress people. It makes them think I've got money, at least.

They don't need to know that I am no City trader or banking executive. In reality, I was then and still am now, a lowly cashier in a bank that happens to be in London. I could have progressed up the food chain but my lack of appetite for added stress and longer hours has kept me at my relatively junior level.

Our branch is a very female-dominated workplace. Other than me, Jezz (sorry, *Jeremy*) is the only man to work there. On any ordinary day I would consider working with women to be a plus, but on my first day back after Mum's death, despite them doing their best to support me through my loss, I wasn't feeling it.

Virginia was the first person I saw as I made my way in through the heavy security doors. She blocked my path and wrapped her arms around me.

Vee would be your stereotypical dumb blonde if it wasn't for her nigh on jet-black hair. She has her annoying traits, but the bank would certainly be a duller place to work without her. On her first day with us a couple of years ago, she took offence at her nameplate. 'I don't want to be Virginia.'

'Why not?' As her 'work buddy', it had been my job to show her the ropes.

'It sounds too much like virgin.'

'Or vagina,' Jezz, still one of the worker bees in those days, helpfully chipped in.

'Call me Vee.'

Vee and I have a bit of history together. We ended up snogging at last year's work summer party. If you put the taste and smell of cigarettes to one side, the snogging was OK. The bit that wasn't OK was hearing Vee telling all the customers about it the following day. From that day on, behind her back at least, Jezz had christened her Virginia the Virgin.

On my first day back, Virginia spent the whole day spouting off to the customers about Mum's death. Each time she mentioned it, she would add in a new embellishment. Early doors, Mr Panchal got off lightly when he was given the news that Mum had died of cancer. By lunchtime Miss Henderson patiently put up with hearing about Mum's 'terrible pain' as she lay 'wasting away' on her deathbed. And as the afternoon slog was drawing to a close, Mrs Jenkins was forced to listen to a full-on Greek tragedy.

'Virginia, will you give it a rest,' I snapped as she was carping on.

'Dave, be a love and call me Vee.'

Shrugging, I tuned Vee out and got on with my work.

I pitied Vee's customers that day. To be fair, mine weren't having a barrel of laughs either. I normally do my best to draw a smile out of the people who grace my counter, but on my first day back, anyone coming in to get money out would have got more personality out of the cashpoint than they did out of me.

That evening, with no band practice to distract me, I spent a couple of hours in my dingy garage, playing a few childhood favourites that reminded me of Mum. Squeeze's 'Pulling Mussels', and, of course, 'Baker Street' were right up there in the Fazackerley hall of fame. Playing 'Baker Street' with Mum was one of my fondest childhood memories.

As the days passed, my thoughts were increasingly drawn to the thorny subject of my maternal parentage. Gazing at the damp brick wall opposite, I started doing a Graham. Maybe I was left on my parents' doorstep one morning by some poor, drug-addled and desperate teenage single mum. Or perhaps I had a surrogate mother. Did they do that sort of thing in the 70s?

I even wondered if Dad was actually my dad at times. Everything I thought I knew about my life was called into question after reading Mum's letter.

But even in my most questioning moments, I would conclude that I am my dad's son. We are peas in a pod. We have similar personalities. Dad's a grumpy old man, slightly ruder than me. I'm a grumpy middle-aged man who just lacks the guts to speak his mind like Dad. Physically, both of us are tall, well-built and pretty much bald. We both shave our heads now, although we both had thick, dark hair in our younger days. I would describe us as tall, dark and handsome but I don't want to blow my own trumpet. Or more to the point, I don't want to blow Dad's trumpet.

My only way of getting answers to the questions floating around in my head was to talk to Dad. My reluctance to discuss Mum's letter with him was partly due to me taking my time to come to terms with Mum's bombshell, but it was also because I didn't want to intrude upon Dad's grief. He had lost his life partner, the woman he had shared a house with and the maker of his hot chocolate.

Sitting in my garage that evening, I knew the time had come to pull my finger out and broach the subject of my birth mother with Dad. Just as I was reaching for my phone, it sprang into action of its own accord. It wasn't Dad though. It was Laura Andrews.

I'd met Laura at St George's hospital earlier that summer. She was a nurse. I was on the bone marrow register and had been called in to donate. It was her job, amongst other things, to stimulate my bone marrow to produce more stem cells so that they could then be extracted and used to help someone beat leukaemia.

Laura stimulated more than my stem cells. Once my week of hospital trips came to an end, Laura and

I had started playing tennis together at the Raynes Park David Lloyd club. We moved on to doing other things together too.

I wouldn't say Laura was my girlfriend. No declaration of undying love was made, no exclusivity deal struck. Neither of us was throwing ourselves unconditionally into the relationship. After an initial intense period, we had settled into a routine of meeting for tennis about once a fortnight, usually on a Wednesday night.

'I'm at the club. Where are you?' Laura asked once the introductory pleasantries were dispensed with. I hadn't even realised it was the first Wednesday of the month.

'Sorry, Laura,' I mumbled. An awkward silence ensued. I was frantically searching for something more substantive to say. The best I could come up with at such short notice was, 'Do you mind if we don't meet tonight?'

'What is it this time? Has your cat died a horrible death?'

'No, but my mother has.' I hadn't told her in the past because when I was with her, the last thing I wanted was sympathy.

'Oh my God, I'm sorry,' Laura said, making me feel bad. I hadn't intended my remark to sound so stark.

In view of my new life goal of winning Lou back, I wanted to end it with Laura, but after I had been overly abrupt with her, I didn't have the heart. I hung up after making vague promises to meet up in a few weeks.

I didn't have the heart to phone Dad in the end,

either. Instead, I found Jezz's half-drunk bottle of Jack Daniels and spent the rest of the evening playing melancholy 70s drudge.

Luckily for me, the band had agreed to meet more often in the run-up to our Raynes Park impromptu gig. We needed the practice, and I needed a distraction to stop me driving myself mad thinking about my mother.

The week before our intended performance, I arranged a Sunday morning rehearsal. My Rectory Close neighbours weren't too impressed with the early start. Luckily Doris, my immediate neighbour, was hard of hearing so she didn't complain too much.

I deliberately called for the early start because it maximised the likelihood that Jezz would be sober. Jezz didn't hit the bottle but that isn't to say he was sober either. He arrived with his greasy hair sticking out at odd angles. His tie-dye shirt hadn't seen an iron in months and he could have carried his shopping home in the bags under his eyes. He looked a total wreck.

Our drummer took great delight in telling us he hadn't been home since the previous day. He tried to imply he had pulled while out clubbing in Sutton, but judging by the unholy mixture of cigarette smoke, alcohol fumes and stale sweat hovering above his drum kit, he probably just got drunk, missed the last bus home and fell asleep on a bench in Nonsuch Park. Outside work, Jezz definitely behaves more like a drummer than a bank manager.

Band practice that morning was a total disaster. You can't play if your drummer stops and holds his head every time he gets to a fill in.

We also had an audience for much of this shambles of a practice. Graham and Amy, his girlfriend, came to watch us rehearse. After a particularly gruesome rendition of Dead or Alive's 'You Spin Me Round', Amy muttered to me under her breath, 'Is that the best drummer you can find? My gran could do a better job than him and she's had Parkinson's disease for the last twenty years.'

Unfortunately, despite having his head in his hands, Jezz heard Amy. He tossed his brushes on the floor and stormed out without saying a word. There endeth our practice.

Jezz was still in a foul mood the following day at work. He accosted me at the coffee machine and told me he didn't want Graham 'and his one-eyed bitch of a girlfriend' coming to any more of our practices. The reference to her one eye was a bit harsh, and I told him so.

'If I am really that bad then maybe I should jack it all in and go somewhere where people appreciate me,' Jezz moaned.

'Don't do that; we love what you do,' I said with as much sincerity as I could muster on a Monday morning at work.

'Yes we do,' agreed Vee, who had walked into the kitchen, unnoticed by either of us. 'You might not be the best boss in the world, Jeremy, and you make some wrong decisions from time to time, but I'm sure with a bit more training you'll get there eventually.'

Jay and I pulled out nearly all the stops to get Jezz to turn up for our last couple of practices before the Sunday gig. I say 'nearly all' because I drew the line at adding 'In the Air Tonight' to the set list. We did play a Thompson Twins song though, so we had a contented drummer again by the end of the practice.

The night before our busk, I dreamed that everything had gone pear-shaped and our gig was a shambles. In my dream it was pissing down with rain, engineering work was stopping trains from coming through the station and Raynes Park was a ghost town.

When I woke up, I was relieved to see the sun creating a luminescent strip on my wall through the gap in the curtains. A quick check on my train app reassured me that they weren't digging up the track this weekend either. The forecourt in front of the station would be busy.

Raynes Park isn't exactly on the cool people's map of London. Nothing exciting ever happens here. It is a place where middle-aged, middle-class people with large middles live. Controversy in Raynes Park is crossing the road somewhere other than at the traffic lights. We have a Waitrose, don't you know.

We didn't have a clue how the good people of RP were going to react to a bunch of us turning up and disturbing their peaceful Sunday afternoon stroll. I for one was feeling slightly petrified as I showered and dressed. If this went tits up, would I ever be able to show my face in the coffee shop, or the bakery, or more to the point, the RPT again? I wasn't frightened of us being abused or attacked or anything like that. My biggest fear was that people would just go about their business without giving a shit. It was that they wouldn't even stop to listen.

Life in the Faz Lane met up at my place for mid-morning bacon sandwiches and coffees before a quick last-minute rehearsal of the five tunes we were planning to play for the masses.

Our set list was 'You Spin Me Round', 'Hold Me Now', 'Where the Streets Have No Name', 'Let's Dance' and finally 'Radio Gaga' – as close as I was prepared to get to 'Bohemian Rhapsody'.

Our run-through went well, although it was interrupted at one point by a phone call from my uncle Robin, Jay's dad. 'Jason told me about your idea for the gig in Raynes Park,' he said. 'Great idea, just make sure my son doesn't get arrested.'

My idea? It was Jay's bloody idea and if there were to be any arrests, it would be Jay's fault.

After a quick snifter of JD, we loaded up Jay's van and drove down to the station. We hadn't thought about where we would park. In the end we had to carry our gear under the pedestrian bridge. It took us ages to set up.

A few of our loyal friends were there for the craic – Graham, Amy and their respective kids, Ray, Boring Bren and mine and Jay's dads. Jay claims to have more than a thousand followers on Twitter but despite him tweeting about this event incessantly for the past week, none of his naked selfie girls turned up.

As soon as we were good to go, we just launched straight in. By the end of our first number, there were probably fifty spectators. One man sitting outside Starbucks told us to piss off so he could drink his coffee in peace, but generally the reaction was really positive. Our U2 rendition had people coming out of the Raynes Park Tavern to listen, or was it just that they needed a fag? I was surprised to see Lou exit the pub too. She had the book dork with her but she waved to me when he wasn't looking.

As we finished the fifth and last tune, a pretty decent rendition of 'Radio Gaga' even if I do say so myself, there were loads more people watching. We even had the top deck of the number 131 bus clapping along while the bus was stuck in a traffic jam. Dad later likened it to something out of a Cliff Richard film. We won't feature that quote on any future marketing material.

'We are Life in the Faz Lane, thank you for sharing your Sunday afternoon with us. The beers are on us,' I foolishly signed off with.

Once I had blown a month's salary in the Tavern and made several mental notes never to speak again during a gig, my fellow band members and I found a table and congratulated ourselves on a job well done. We were buzzing. 'We should have sold merchandise,' Jay commented.

'And CDs,' was Jezz's contribution. I didn't bother pointing out that we didn't possess any of either.

Jezz was banging on about some woman giving him her phone number. Graham's son Sean brought us back down to earth a bit, though. 'Don't you know anything that isn't, like, so old?' he asked as he was leaving the pub with his dad.

Even Dad thought we did well. 'That was top stuff, our kid,' he told me once he had got his Cliff Richard quip off his chest, 'well done.' It might not sound much, but from my dad, that was serious praise. He has high standards when it comes to music and definitely isn't easy to please.

I just wish Mum had been there to see it.

Chapter Four

The buzz from the live shindig lasted for a while. It even included a few mentions on Wandsworth Radio and Radio Jackie, our local stations. Eventually though, the glow faded and my mind again began to drift back towards my maternal situation.

Nearly a month after Mum's death, once I had run out of excuses not to, I phoned Dad and invited myself to dinner.

Mum and Dad, just Dad now, lived in a bog-standard terraced house on a tree-lined road in the cultural wasteland that is Morden. To distinguish the house from the structurally identical houses surrounding it, my individualistic mum had insisted on a light green New England-style exterior paint job and a multi-coloured crazy paving drive. 'Mutton dressed as lamb,' Dad had christened the house's appearance even before the second coat of green paint had dried.

This wasn't the first time I had visited Dad since Mum's funeral but it was the first time I had gone with the specific intention of asking him about the letter. It wasn't every day you got to ask your dad who your mum was. I was sweating as I rang the electronic bell.

'I haven't got around to getting rid of that shit yet,' Dad said upon answering the door. He might have been referring to the green paint, the crazy paving or even the tinny and water-damaged burst that had once been their 'Ride of the Valkyries' doorbell.

As he stood aside to let me in, I saw Mum's bright red fleece occupying pride of place on the bannister. Dad had done absolutely nothing with the house since Mum's death. It still bore all the hallmarks of being her place. 'I'm not keeping it there as some sort of shrine,' he said as he saw me smiling at the fleece. 'I was just bloody cold the other day and couldn't find mine.'

Dad looked OK. He was clean shaven and had even shaved his scalp, something he often neglected until Mum would take the piss. Even his shirt was ironed. He was showing no physical signs of falling apart without Mum. 'I'm doing alright, our kid,' was his verdict on his welfare, and I couldn't find a reason to disagree.

While Dad was chatting about life without Mum, he was draining vegetables and putting the finishing touches to our lunch. I had rarely eaten food prepared by Dad before. Mum always did the cooking, right up until the last few days when her cancer made it difficult for her to walk. Credit to Dad though, he actually managed to produce an edible meat and two veg.

As we ate in their farmhouse-style kitchen looking out onto the garden, we chatted about Mum, the funeral and the future. At one point I asked Dad what he was going to do with her clothes. 'I'm going to leave them all where they are. You can chuck the lot out when I die,' he told me. Thanks, Dad.

Over a pot of tea after our dinner, I plucked up the courage to broach the subject of the day. Much as I was tempted to, I didn't just ask him outright who my mother was. Instead I told him about the letter.

'I know she wrote to you,' he told me. 'She wrote to me too.' He got up, rummaged through a kitchen drawer and handed me a similar-looking letter to the one I had at home.

Dear Terry,

I guess I've popped my clogs now. Either that or you're ignoring my instruction not to read this until I've died. It wouldn't be the first time you've not listened to me, would it ,you daft old sod.

You know you mean the world to me. We've had a great life together. I'm guessing I won't be around quite long enough to celebrate our forty-fifth wedding anniversary but we've had a decent run.

When I first met you, at that Fairport Convention gig on Parliament Hill, despite being soaked to the skin in that awful weather, you were the most hip man there. I'll never forget watching you do your stuff with your fancy guitar, wearing your bell-bottomed jeans and that ridiculous headband.

You introduced me to all the band members and to the guys from Jefferson Airplane. None of them were half as good-looking as you though. Somehow, I knew from the first moment I saw you that we were meant to be together.

It hasn't always been plain sailing though, has it? We had our tricky time but we got over it. And we have David to show for it. David, our son.

We've often discussed telling David our secret. At first, I desperately wanted him to see me as his real mother. I didn't want him feeling insecure about my love for him. And then, the longer we left it without him knowing, the harder it became to tell him.

As I lie here with my strength ebbing away, it has struck me that it would be so awful if David's birth mother contacted him after we'd both died. He wouldn't have the chance to ask us about our secret. He would feel totally let down and betrayed. We can't let that happen.

I hope you'll forgive me but I've taken matters into my own hands. I've written to David, telling him how proud we are of him and how much we love him. When was the last time we actually told him that? I've also told David that I'm not his real mother. I didn't give him the whole story. I know more of the full story than you think, but I'm sure I don't know everything.

You'll need to prepare yourself for a conversation with David. Be honest with him. Tell him everything. It makes me sad to say it, but I know you haven't been totally honest with me.

As I'm writing this, I can hear the children playing in the school playground at the end of the garden. In the grand scheme of things, life goes on. You're still fit and healthy. Don't mope around. Get out and enjoy the rest of your life. I wouldn't mind if you got together with Debbie next door. She's always had a thing for you and if I'm not mistaken, she's been sniffing at your scent for a while already.

Remember, I left you detailed instructions on

how to work the washing machine. Even though
I'm on my deathbed I can't stop worrying about the
state of your clothes.
I love you always,
Val
x

Dad and I sat there for a while, lost in our own thoughts. In time, I looked up at him. He might well have had a shave and ironed his clothes, but, sitting across from him, I noticed he was looking a bit older. His normally tanned skin looked pale. His eyes were almost lost amidst the worry lines and puffiness. The loss of a loved one will do that to someone but I couldn't help wondering whether the thought of having to have this conversation with me had added impetus to Dad's ageing process. Deep and meaningful didn't come easily to Dad.

Eventually, trying valiantly to hold back the tears, Dad spoke.

'I had an affair,' he started hesitantly while staring at the scratches on the oak dining table. 'I had an affair with a singer called Sue. She was from New Zealand. We met when I was doing some session work. Your mother was touring with yet another jazz band and I was on my own. The affair didn't last long.'

He got up from the table to grab a box of tissues from the worktop, blew his nose and returned to his seat.

'I woke up one morning and felt incredibly guilty. I thought what the fuck am I doing and ended it there and then. I was so relieved once it was over. It was like a huge weight had been lifted off my shoulders. She didn't get in touch for ages after that. I was convinced the whole thing was behind me.'

'But it wasn't,' I prompted when Dad didn't carry on.

'It wasn't, no. One morning Val and I were sitting here eating our breakfast when the doorbell rang. Val went to answer it. There she was, standing on our doorstep holding a baby. I didn't even know she was pregnant.'

Bloody hell. Now it was my turn to get up and pace around. Dad sat still, his hands wrapped around his now cold cup of tea. I couldn't think straight. Images of Mum standing there, face to face with Dad's temporary shag, his other woman, someone who Mum hadn't even known existed until that moment, were flashing through my head. Images of this woman with a baby.

'What did you do?' I eventually asked.

'Your mother called me to the door. Sue handed you over to me and that was it, we never saw her again.'

'She just handed me over? Didn't she say anything?'

'She told me you were born on 9th January. Then she said, "He's yours." That was it.'

Dad went on to tell me that he and Mum hadn't been able to have children of their own. The two of them had been trying for ages. 'Your mother blamed me for our lack of success in the baby department. She'd say things like, "If only your loins were as fertile as your imagination, we'd have a houseful of screaming brats by now."'

Dad sat back, looked up at the ceiling and blew out his cheeks. He was clearly relieved that his secret was out.

As well as thinking about how Mum must have felt, I couldn't help feeling for Dad. Yes, he was the one who had the affair when he was younger. But who was I to judge Dad for something he had done forty-plus years ago? I am not whiter than white myself. As he was talking, he looked lost, totally unsure of himself. He struggled to look me in the eye, and when he did manage to focus on me, all I could see in his expression was uncertainty, maybe even shame.

Because my hands needed something to do, I got my phone out and googled 'Sue, singer, New Zealand'. More than a million results came up. Dad leaned over to see what was occupying my gaze.

'She went by Sue, but don't forget she could have been a Susan, or a Suzie,' he threw into the mix. 'Sue might even just have been her stage name for all I know.'

'What? How the hell do I find her if that's the case?'

'I guess you don't.'

'This is bullshit.' I made no attempt to hide my frustration. 'If you know so little about her, how do you know she wasn't shagging someone else at the same time she was shagging you?'

'I think I would have noticed if there were three of us in the bed, don't you?'

'Stop being a twat, Dad.' I snatched up my phone and showed him a few of the photos Google had so co-operatively provided me with. 'Was that her?' I pointed to a picture of a chubby red-head with a microphone in her mouth.

'Don't be soft, lad.' Dad shook his head and stood up. I stood up too. Dad's awkwardness and seedy revelations were getting on my nerves. We were barely civil to each other as I got my coat and headed out of the front door.

As I walked the mile or so home, I thought of Mum. She never did have a child of her own, in the biological sense at least. Despite getting the shock of her life that morning, somehow she forgave Dad for his indiscretion. She had also been able to treat me as if I was hers. That must have taken her some time to come to terms with.

Grabbing a bottle of lager when I got home, I went into my garage and started playing 'Your Song' by Elton John. My heart wasn't in it though, so in the end I just sat drinking in the dimming light.

My thoughts were eventually interrupted by the sound of the Divinyls singing 'I Touch Myself'. Some smartarse, probably Jay, had been messing with my phone.

It was Graham. 'So who's your BM then?' he asked when I answered the call.

I filled him in on my conversation with Dad.

'My money's on that Kiwi opera bird,' he said before signing off.

Chapter Five

After talking to Dad about my birth mother, I decided to push my luck and see if I could make progress in my other life goal, reigniting the spark between Lou and me.

After the way we broke up, it was a miracle we were even talking again now, let alone thinking about getting back together. Well, at least one of us was thinking about it.

Before Lou ran off with the book dork, if anyone had asked me what I thought of my marriage, I would have told them how happy Lou and I were. Sure, the novelty of each other's company had generally worn off, but we were happy. We went out together when the mood took us, we didn't row about who did the washing up and we still laughed at each other's jokes. Well, she laughed at mine at least.

The first time I can remember even getting an inkling that Lou might not share my view of the state of our marriage was one night when I was watching the football on the telly. 'Not football again. Do you have to watch that crap tonight?'

'There aren't any period dramas on tonight, it's a Tuesday,' I told her. I wasn't necessarily sure my statement held true, but the football was tense so

I did my best to sound convincing.

'I don't want to watch the telly. It would be nice if we could have a conversation from time to time.'

'We are having a conversation, aren't we?'

'No, I'm talking to you and you're watching the football. That's hardly having a conversation. We don't stimulate each other anymore.'

That got my attention. 'You stimulate me, darling.'

'Not physical stimulation, Dave, mental stimulation.'

To my shame, I sighed with relief and turned back to watch the Liverpool game.

The next thing I knew, Lou had committed us to attending a book club. She went to the library after work one night and picked up two copies of the Cobham linguists' book of the month, *The Book Thief* by Markus Zusak.

Now I can read a book as much as the next man. There is nothing better than a gripping whodunit or a meaty courtroom drama. But, since studying Shakespeare at school, dissecting the author's motives for taking the plot in one direction or another has never been my cup of tea. I couldn't even understand Shakespeare, let alone critique the development of his characters.

Not wanting to upset Lou, one sunny evening in May, I traipsed along to some double-fronted mansion in deepest Surrey to talk about *The Book Thief*. Lou and I, along with six or seven middle-aged white women called Emily and Olivia, and one bloke with an unruly beard that seemed to morph at about neck level into a brown cardigan, were shown into a conservatory looking onto a garden as big as a golf course. Feeling irritated that my free time was being taken up by this crap, I grabbed a chair overlooking the garden. If nothing else, at least I could enjoy the view.

My mood improved no end when our host for the evening, Bernadette, started opening the wine. I fancied a lager but she didn't have any, so I opted for the red. Even the crisps were a cut above those served at your average Raynes Park house party.

'So, what did you think of the book?' my new friend Bernie asked to kick proceedings off. Having given up my evening for this, I was as anxious to express my opinion as everyone else. We all spoke at once.

'It was remarkable.'

'Stunningly vivid.'

'Story-telling at its best.'

'Fabulous portrayal of attitudes.'

'A bit long.'

Luckily for me, Bernie didn't turn to me first to elaborate on my insight. Instead she asked Mr Beard, later to become known as the book dork, why he had found it so 'stunningly vivid'.

Listening to pretentious drivel isn't one of my strengths. Mr Beard's use of phrases like 'evocative symbolism' and 'enlightening soliloquies' soon had me clamouring for more wine.

By the time Bernie did come to me, I had drunk most of the contents of her two-hundred-year-old wine cellar and could only just remember what we were supposed to be talking about. 'It wasn't the best book I have ever read, Bernie,' I began.

'Bunny.'

'I beg your pardon?'

'If you must shorten my name, it's Bunny, not Bernie.'

'Sorry, Bunny.'

'Thank you. Now feel free to tell us why it wasn't the best book you have ever read.'

'Listen, this book starts off with a load of complete drivel and goes downhill from there. It's just pretentious bollocks, the author's up his own arse. I'm sure there's a great story in there somewhere, but couldn't the writer just tell it from start to finish in a normal way rather than trying to be clever?'

'Ah, so you didn't like the idea of Death as the omniscient narrator of the novel then? And please refrain from using bad language. It offends my sensitivities.'

'Shit, sorry, Bunny.'

'Bernadette.'

'Bernadette.'

'Did you even finish the book?' Mr Beard chipped in.

'Of course I finished the fucking book.'

'What happened then?'

'He died.'

'Who died?' Lou jumped on the bandwagon.

'I don't know, the bad guy?' I hadn't finished the book. I hadn't got beyond the pretentious introduction. Lou didn't utter a word to me as she drove us home that night.

And that was the start of the ignominy that was to escalate when I witnessed the book dork kissing my wife at New Malden station a few weeks later and then conclude with him turning up in his Ford Ka to help her move her stuff out. 'What, are you taking one pair of knickers at a time?' I asked when I saw his car pull up outside.

'I'm not taking my knickers,' my soon-to-be ex replied, 'I won't be wearing them much.'

Two years on, I was under no illusions. Winning Lou back wasn't going to be easy. The more I thought about it, the more I realised I needed a plan. Walking up to her and saying, 'Hey, babe, I have always loved you. Move back in with me,' was a plan of sorts, but its chances of success were slim at best. I needed something more nuanced, more involved, more grown-up.

So Project Lou was born.

Writing out a full-blown project plan would have been sad in the extreme, so on the way home from work one Tuesday night, I confined myself to jotting down a few actions that, if followed, could increase my chances of spending the rest of my life with Lou.

1   Stop playing the field.
2   Appeal to Lou's romantic side. Show her she wants to be with me after all.
3   Show her I'm an intellectual. Have grown-up conversations, about politics, philosophy and the arts.
4   If the above fails, murder the book dork.

Politicians might have called my list a road map to love or a four point peace plan. Graham would have called it pathetic. But to me, enacting this plan, with the possible exception of number four, was more important than finding my birth mother.

After writing my list and filing it at the bottom of my man drawer in the kitchen (I had no intention of ever showing it to anyone, especially Graham) I decided to take a couple of immediate steps to put my plan into action. The first of which was to phone Laura.

'Oh hi, Dave,' she said upon answering, 'I was going to phone you. Do you fancy meeting up next week? You could take me shopping.'

Regaining control of the conversation was my priority. 'I'm sorry, Laura, but there's a lot going on in my life at the moment, what with my mother dying and everything. I'm not feeling it. Maybe we should call it quits between us?'

'Are you sure that's what you want?' There was a bit of an edge to her voice.

I tried to soften my tone a bit to let her down gently. 'We did have some great times, on and off the tennis court.'

'Your forehand isn't bad but your foreplay leaves a lot to be desired.'

'I don't remember you moaning at the time.'

'Exactly, Dave, exactly,' she said before ending the call. I let her cheap shot ride. If she put the phone down with a smile on her face then good for her.

That was step one sorted. Steps two and three required some interaction with Lou. I thought about putting talking to Lou off until another day, but I could hear Mum's voice in my ear. 'Take control. Strike while the iron's hot.'

I called my ex-wife. 'Have dinner with me,' I said when she answered.

'Why?'

'Because.'

After a short pause, Lou was won over by my charm. We agreed to meet in La Mamma in Worcester Park. Project Lou was going great guns.

I wasn't unduly surprised that Lou agreed to meet

me. Despite the animosity that had threatened to drown us when she shacked up with the book dork, the two of us had been back on speaking terms for a while now. We even slept together around the time that Mum's cancer was confirmed as being terminal. With hindsight, I'm sure Lou just felt sorry for me. She soon 'came to her senses' as she described it and knocked our sex on the head.

Lou insisted on meeting straight after work rather than later in the evening when the staff light the candles and dim the spots. That was probably her way of telling me she wanted a friendly dinner rather than a romantic night out. Step two of Project Lou demanded romance. I had my work cut out.

Whole books have been written on how to reignite a romance. Sitting in La Mamma waiting for Lou to turn up, I couldn't help wishing I had read some of them.

It wasn't that I didn't do romance – I proposed to Lou in Paris on Valentine's Day. Even that didn't go without a hitch though. I had wanted to go for a glass of Dutch courage in a street café to start off our day trip but Lou insisted on visiting the Louvre. She fell down the steps outside the gallery so instead of spending a couple of hours gazing at Da Vinci's masterpieces, we spent the rest of the day looking at X-rays of Lou's broken ankle.

I had planned to propose to Lou at the top of the Eiffel Tower, with France's capital glowing seductively in the setting sun around us, but in the end I got down on one knee as the love of my life was sipping a medicinal brandy on the plane home. 'Lou, will you marry me?'

'Sir, get back in your seat, please, the seatbelt sign's still on.'

Lou was familiar with my romantic side. She just hadn't seen it for a while. To help get her into the right mood in La Mamma, when the waiter came to take my drinks order, I asked him to light the candle.

The beers were on the table by the time Lou arrived. As always she looked stunning, in a simple black dress that looked a bit risqué for a work outfit.

'I've come straight from an awards ceremony,' she told me when I asked her about it. 'You have to dress up for these things.'

'You look hot.' Her blonde hair shone in the candlelight.

'Geoff thinks it makes me look frumpy.'

'Geoff's a dick.'

As she was tucking into her linguini and I was twirling spaghetti clumsily around my fork, I told her my news about Mum not being my real mum. Unlike everyone else I had told, Lou didn't gasp upon hearing the news. She didn't take the piss either. We talked about the various connotations for a while, but my heart wasn't really in that conversation.

Once the waitress had placed Irish coffees where our plates had been, I plucked up the courage to move the conversation on to more intimate subjects.

'Why did we really split up?'

'Do we have to go over old ground,' she asked, although with no hint of frustration in her voice.

'It's just such a waste.'

'Of what?' my ex asked. She was looking at me intently. Something in her expression encouraged me to go on.

'Of our lives. I've always loved you. Move back in with me.' So much for the nuanced, grown-up approach.

'Oh, Dave, don't ask me to do that.' A tear slid down her cheek, gleaming in the candlelight.

'Why not?' I leaned forward a little more, closing the gap between us. Lou took the bait and kissed me. It was long, hard and passionate, just like old times.

Eventually she pulled away and stood up. As she gathered up her handbag and jacket, she wouldn't meet my gaze. It was only once she had put her jacket on that she turned to face me. 'I can't do this again,' she stammered, before turning and fleeing from the restaurant.

I sat there for a while, reflecting upon the evening and finishing off Lou's Irish coffee. As always when I spent time with Lou, I felt alive. Despite her refusal to move back in with me – an offer I hadn't meant to make – our kiss, which I knew would stay with me for weeks, gave me a lot of encouragement.

The only disappointing thing about the evening was that I hadn't got the chance to talk to Lou about the crisis in the Middle East and how the West might support local people to defeat Isis, a subject I had been reading up on in preparation for our dinner. I made a mental note to prioritise point three of Project Lou the next time the two of us met.

Once I had paid the bill, I went home and played 'Louise' by Human League over and over again. The lyrics were so apt, they could have been written for our situation.

Chapter Six

As celebrations go, birthdays in the Fazackerley household are only a short way behind Christmas in their importance. The routine on the evening of the anniversary of Mum's birth had remained similar over the years. The family and a select band of friends would go to a swanky restaurant and eat, drink and laugh the night away. Mum would turn up in some outlandish but somehow stylish outfit, Dad would be drunk before the sweet trolley made its appearance and I would be lumbered with getting the pissed old man home without him sustaining serious alcohol-related injuries.

This year, Mum's birthday fell on a Saturday. Instead of raucous laughter, stylish dresses and a drunk dad, there was me and my piano. I missed Mum.

By lunchtime, my garage walls were closing in on me. Wondering how Dad was remembering Mum on her special day, I decided to pay him an impromptu visit.

Alerting Dad to my imminent arrival didn't seem necessary. As far as I knew, he never went anywhere. He was bound to be in, sitting listening to The Stones or The Who or something else from his vast vinyl collection.

I pressed the bell that set the Valkyries stumbling and gurgling, if not riding. No one came to the door. Fiddling with my key ring, it took me a while to find the key to my childhood home. After a few false starts, I got the right one and let myself in. Dad was coming down the stairs in his dressing gown. 'God, Dad, you can't just lie in bed all day,' I launched in. 'Just because Mum died, you shouldn't be moping around as though your life has ended.'

Dad was about to reply when the next-door neighbour appeared at the top of the stairs wearing one of Dad's old-man check shirts. In itself, there was nothing remarkable about her wearing dad's shirt, but the shirt was all she was wearing. And it was totally unbuttoned. Bloody hell.

'What are you doing here?' Dad asked, his voice taking on a higher pitch than normal.

'Christ, Dad,' was all I could say.

Recovering quickly as Debbie beat a hasty retreat back into the bedroom, Dad invited me to join him for a post-coital cup of tea. I declined his kind offer and beat a hasty retreat myself.

It should have been Mum in that house with Dad. Whereas I had spent the morning playing music that would have pleased Mum, Dad was more interested in pleasing the next-door neighbour. True, Mum did give him permission to attach himself to Debbie, but I don't suppose she thought he would do it so quickly. Bearing in mind Dad's previous form, I shouldn't have been surprised though.

With Dad shagging the neighbour, I felt the need to cleanse myself by spending some time with Mum on her birthday. I went home, grabbed Jay's guitar from my garage and drove up Grand Drive to the cemetery.

As I made my way along the gun-barrel straight road that dissects the sprawling expanse of stones, flowers and grass within the cemetery's borders, I passed a few people spending quiet moments with their departed loved ones. Not feeling particularly sociable, I was relieved to see the graves in the vicinity of Mum's plot were deserted except for the occasional pigeon.

Mum's headstone hadn't been installed yet. Her plot looked nondescript and bare when compared to those surrounding it. That didn't help my mood. Neither did the big droplets of rain that began falling from the darkening skies as I sat down on the kerb beside Mum's grave.

Playing Mum a few of her favourite tunes felt like the right thing to do. Though the guitar isn't my instrument, I had managed to pick up more than the basics. Dad considered knowing the difference between a single coil and a humbucker as an essential part of my life education.

I was absorbed in my memories and midway through 'Stairway to Heaven' when Graham's ex-wife tapped me on the shoulder. My heart nearly missed a beat. Helen lived in their former marital home, the back garden of which backs onto the cemetery. Over the years, I have spent a fair bit of time in the same social circle as Helen. We weren't close, but we weren't distant either. She could be a bit needy at times, but as I was discovering, so could I.

Helen and I sat chatting across Mum's grave. She knew about Mum's battle with cancer. She didn't know about Dad doing it doggy style with Debbie on the dining table. She laughed when I dropped that titbit into the conversation.

'How can you laugh? It isn't funny,' I said a bit stuffily. 'That image of Debbie showing me all she has will stay with me forever.'

'Oh come on, Dave, you don't want your dad to be miserable for the rest of his life, do you?'

'No, but five minutes of misery on Mum's birthday isn't too much to ask, is it?'

'What was the first thing you did when you and Louise broke up?'

'Burn my library books.'

'Knowing you as I do, Mr F,' Helen pontificated, 'I bet you went out and found yourself another woman. Am I right?'

She was right. I had slept with one of Lou's work colleagues, more to make a point to Lou than to myself. A sort of 'look what you're missing' point. I wasn't proud of that particular indiscretion and didn't confess it to Helen, but she could tell from the look on my face that she had scored a hit. 'When Louise left you, you had to prove you still had it,' she continued. 'I bet that's all your dad's doing.'

Helen eventually got up to leave. Her parting shot as she strode down the path was, 'Maybe you should have some of what your dad's drinking.' The sky was even darker by then, but I could have sworn she winked at me as she walked off.

I shook my head, more to release a bit of tension than to disagree with anything in particular. It occurred to me that I didn't tell Helen about Mum not being my mum during our graveside chat. In the lead-up to Mum's birthday, to show respect for Mum, I had deliberately pushed my questionable maternal parentage to the back of my mind. Dad, on the other hand, had afforded Mum no respect at all.

Before leaving the cemetery I told Mum of my determination to find my birth mother.

Over the days that followed, I allowed myself to begin considering the myriad of questions that had been lurking at the back of my mind for weeks. What was her full name? Why did she leave me with Dad? Has she regretted it since? What was she like? Was she rich? I wasn't proud of that last thought and tried not to dwell on it, but it was there amongst the others in the jumble that was my mind.

How well did Dad really know this Sue? How did he know I was definitely his? What if Sue had been putting it about a bit? My dad might be some tall, dark, handsome roadie.

My anger with Dad made me less prepared to take his word at face value. The more I thought about it, the more convinced I became that he was hiding something from me.

Another conversation was called for. This time I phoned him up on my way home from work as I couldn't face walking in on him and Debbie again.

As soon as he picked up the phone, I jumped straight in.

'I've had enough of this crap. You're going to help me find Sue.'

Part Two

Terry Fazackerley

Chapter Seven

Breathing is something you generally take for granted, but as I invited our kid into my house for the pre-arranged maternity summit on a cold Thursday evening in November, I had to remind myself to inhale. I was dead nervous.

I always knew that when he was ready, David would want to know more about his real mother. I couldn't blame him for that. As Debbie often pointed out when I discussed it with her, anyone in David's position would want to know the truth.

I looked at my boy as he sat opposite me at our old kitchen table. He is a handsome man, dark-skinned with a shaven head and eyes as alert as a hawk's. He definitely inherited most of his looks from me, but other things were more Sue. Whereas I can be a bit uptight and opinionated, he is easy-going and would do anything to avoid a fight. David is much more sociable and lively in a crowd than me. He is a darn sight cleverer than me too.

Val was right, we could be proud of the way our boy has turned out. I love him as much as anyone could love their son, which explains why my task that evening was so hard. I wanted to help him, but so soon after losing Val, I didn't want to shake his faith in his other parent as well.

After reading Val's letter, I spent hours, days even, trying to work out how to tell my story in a way that would satisfy David's curiosity about his birth mother without encouraging him to launch a full-scale search for her. No good could come of that, not for me any road.

Despite all my planning though, as I sipped from my chipped mug of tea with my boy sitting opposite me, I found myself lost for words. I couldn't bring myself to dive straight in, so instead of talking about the events of 1973, I apologised for the awkward incident on Val's birthday. Debbie didn't stop blushing for days afterwards.

My apology momentarily seemed to throw David, but he soon recovered, waving his hand as if to dismiss the subject altogether.

'I was lonely,' I explained, feeling the need to justify my actions. 'I didn't want to be alone.' There was no point in telling David that Debbie and I have been close for quite some time.

'I'm not here to talk about your sex life,' my boy chastised me.

'That's not strictly true,' I corrected him, 'it was my sex life that got us into this position in the first place.'

David was frowning. 'Cut the crap, Dad. Tell me about Sue. How did you meet her? How long were you seeing her for? What was she like?' After he had finished speaking, he put his mug down, leaned forwards and looked directly at me. Every ounce of his being was focussed on getting me to talk about his mother.

Draining my own tea, I closed my eyes and let the memories from 1973 flood back into my mind. After swallowing hard, I told David what I hoped, but didn't necessarily believe, would be enough to satisfy his curiosity.

'In a nutshell, son, Sue was from New Zealand. She came to London to make her way in the music industry. We met at a recording job. We got on, saw each other a few times. One thing led to another and she got pregnant.'

Our kid's frown intensified. 'You've already given me the headline. I want the story, and the unabridged version at that.'

It was going to be a long night. Thinking quickly, I reached a decision. What harm would it do if I was honest about my affair with Sue? It was what happened once the affair had broken up that I needed to blag about.

1973 was a big year for me. Coming into the year, I was busy. As a guitarist I wasn't in the Hendrix, Clapton and Page league. I wasn't famous but I was known on the London music scene. I got to riff with some of the best.

People admired me. I was good-looking, rich and pretty cool too, driving around the streets of London in my signal red Triumph Stag. With my cocksure look and my expensive clobber, I was a somebody. I was probably a bit of a gobshite.

People knew Val too. Val was, if anything, even more successful than me. Bands clamoured to have one of the best sax players in London in their ranks. During the early 1970s, Val travelled around Europe with a host of different groups, making a name for herself and, just as importantly, making money.

We were both busy. Months sometimes went by without us seeing each other. The first half of 1973 was one such time. Early that year, Val caught the ferry to France to begin two back-to-back tours in Europe with some jazz buddies. Most of my work was based at studios in and around London, so I stayed at home.

Sue and I first met at the International Broadcasting Company studios in Portland Place. I was recording with some crappy band hoping to be the next big thing on the glam rock scene. The band's rhythm guitarist had just been given the boot, by all accounts because he was crap. They asked me to fill in until they could find a permanent replacement.

The studios were often populated by far out wannabes dressed in threads no one with an ounce of sense would ever be seen dead in. On that Saturday lunchtime, nothing seemed out of the ordinary as the door was held open for me by a bloke wearing gold flares and a silver jacket. His mates were equally loud in their clobber. A young bird with striking, long, brilliantly red hair and lovely legs nipped in through the door before me. Following her into the studios was an absolute delight.

Mr Gold Flares and his cronies turned out to be my buddies for the afternoon. I had never met anyone in the band before. My manager told me they were a bunch of fruitcakes, but being fruitcakes was almost mandatory in the music business at that time.

Introductions were made. When it came to the girl with the flame hair's turn, she announced in the broadest Antipodean accent I had ever heard, 'I'm

72

Sue. I'm with him,' and gestured towards me. I was too dumbfounded to correct her. She winked at me. I kept my mouth shut, mostly because I was frightened it would drop open and my tongue would hang out.

The recording session turned out to be a shambles. The song we were recording was pure drudge. The lead singer couldn't sing, the drummer was so stoned he didn't know what planet he was on and the lead guitarist was so godawful I couldn't help wondering whether they had sacked the wrong band member. I didn't really give a toss about the quality of the music though. So long as I played what I was told to play, they would pay me, ta very much.

When their studio time ran out, we gathered up our equipment and filed back out onto the street. Just as I had followed her into the studio earlier, I followed the red-head bird out.

The noise of police sirens was the first thing we noticed as we emerged back into the daylight. There were police cars everywhere. The roads seemed to be gridlocked too. The worried looks on the faces of the drivers and pedestrians around us told us that something big was going on. We learned that car bombs had exploded in different parts of London. There could be more out there somewhere. This wasn't an afternoon to be hanging about on the streets.

My car wasn't far away. Sue was heading for the Tube but it didn't seem safe for anyone to be wandering around London so I offered her a lift. There was a Tube strike too that day, so Sue accepted my offer without argument.

With the traffic at a standstill, it took us ages to drive to the Earls Court backpacker hostel Sue was kipping at. During our stop-start journey, and then in the boozer afterwards, Sue told me how she had begged, borrowed and stolen money to fund her trip to England. She was totally convinced she would succeed in making a career out of her singing. Her optimism was nearly as admirable as her arse.

'Can you sing then?' I asked her.

'Can you play the guitar?' She had some spark about her. It was that spark, that infectious energy, that carefree attitude that influenced my decision to buy her another drink that night. Or it could have been the gorgeous flame-coloured hair, the mischievous smile or the tight-fitting black jumper.

Before I knew it, last orders were called and I could hardly remember where I had parked the car. I certainly wasn't capable of driving it home, not even in those days when drink-driving was less of an issue.

'You'll just have to kip on my floor then,' Sue had whispered in a husky voice as she put her arm through mine and steered me towards her hostel.

Needless to say, neither of us slept on the floor that night. Neither of us slept much at all.

When I got to the part where I spent the night with Sue, David felt the need to speak up. 'Spare me the details of the actual act,' he cautioned me. My throat was dry. I used his interruption as an opportunity to grab a drink.

The drinks cabinet was full of vermouth, curaçao and other middle-class crap Val had bought over the years but never used. I was about to grab a bottle of mineral water when I spotted her Christmas present to me from last year, a twenty-year-old single malt, nestled in behind the Harvey's Bristol Cream. This was proper upper-class stuff. David willingly accepted my offer of a glass.

Our kid had listened intently to my description of the day I met Sue. He nodded when I likened myself to an arrogant prick, smiled when I mentioned how much in demand Mum was, but most of the time he was frowning.

'So was it a one-night stand or something more lasting?' he prompted me.

'Something more lasting.' There was no point in blagging. 'From the moment we met, Sue and I were inseparable. We chatted, we laughed, we ate together, we went everywhere together. She made me feel special. We couldn't keep our hands off each other.'

'For God's sake, Dad, you were married.'

David was right of course, I couldn't defend myself. At the time, what I was doing didn't seem real. Val was somewhere in Austria, or was it Germany? It wasn't as if she was waiting for me at home. It wasn't an excuse, but I always knew my time with Sue was temporary. I knew it would end.

Doing my best to water down my descriptions of my attraction to Sue so as to spare David's blushes, I carried on with my account of the events of that spring. This story hadn't been told more than once in the past forty years. In a strange way, it felt good to be getting it off my chest.

Sue accompanied me to numerous recording sessions and gigs over the two-month duration of our affair. The gig that really stands out in my memory is the one that took place on 18th May 1973.

I was made up with myself. Pink Floyd's Dark Side of the Moon album was making a huge splash and

I managed to get my hands on two VIP tickets to see their show at the new Earls Court Arena. I drove into London and met Sue in the afternoon. We spent some time at her digs. She seemed unusually quiet. I didn't think much of it at the time because I was excited at the prospect of seeing my idols.

The gig was awesome. Waters and Gilmour were the height of musical cool. Boy did I want to be them.

I hadn't paid much attention to Sue during the gig, but as we were walking back to her hostel, I noticed she was crying. And that's when she told me she was up the duff.

When I got to that point in the story, David interrupted me as I had expected he would. 'You told me you hadn't known she was pregnant.'

'I know. Sorry, lad,' I said.

'But why did you lie?'

'You've just lost your mother. I wanted to be your rock, but this whole affair makes me look a bit of a shite.' David just shook his head in response.

I emptied my whisky glass. David lifted the bottle but I refused a refill. The story got tricky from here on in and I needed a clear head.

'Sue's words that night outside her hostel were like the proverbial slap in the face,' I explained. 'They were my wake-up call. What the hell had I been doing for the past couple of months? I was a married man after all.'

'I'm glad you remembered at last,' David said.

Ignoring David's interruption, I described how, from the moment Sue told me she was pregnant, everything had changed. Every time I looked at her, I saw Val, hurt and upset. Bluntly, Sue became a problem I needed to resolve. I'm not proud of myself, but that's how I felt. At that time, if I could have erased the events that led to me meeting her, I would have done so without hesitation.

The two of us spent the next few weeks having a series of barneys about what to do next. I didn't want to carry on with our relationship. Sue did. We talked through the various options. We even discussed her having an abortion. I couldn't bring myself to mention that conversation to David though. It hadn't been a very long conversation in any event, going something along the lines of me suggesting it, Sue saying no and punching me in the face.

It all seemed so unfair to me at the time. Val and I had been trying to have a baby for a couple of years, and then Sue came along and conceived within five minutes.

'Hadn't you heard of protection?'

'Nothing I did at that time was particularly sensible,' I told my son as I got myself a glass of council pop.

I went on to tell David how Sue refused to talk to me once she got it into her head that there was no future for us as a couple. She wouldn't answer her door, and when I met her in the street outside her hostel, she just blanked me. Eventually, about a week before Val was due back from Europe, I was in a panic. Things needed to be sorted, so I went to her hostel to confront her.

Sue was struggling for money. I took a bundle of cash with me. If she was going to have the baby, at least she would be able to go back to New Zealand and have it there.

'You were just going to get her out of your life, baby and all,' David asked. I didn't dare tell him that my plan A had still been a termination. Instead, I told him that it didn't matter what I was going to do, because when I got there, Sue had already skedaddled.

David looked straight at me, disapproval etched across his face. Would he ever regain the loving and respectful expression that had previously come naturally to him in my company?

'And the next time you saw her was on your doorstep nine months later?' he asked.

'Yes.' I couldn't look him in the eye at this point. I wasn't proud of myself.

My boy sighed. He was still frustrated. I might have sighed too, with relief that my grilling was coming to an end.

My relief didn't last long though. David wasn't prepared to leave matters there.

'I want to find her,' he said.

I refilled my glass. To hell with a clear head, I needed a bevvy.

Chapter Eight

I didn't want David to meet Sue. What good could come of him jetting off across the world to chase a dream? If Val was right in her opinion that David still loved his ex-wife, then he would be better off devoting his attention to making up with her than chasing after a woman who walked out on him when he was a baby.

Admittedly, I also had some selfish reasons for not wanting the two of them to meet. Sue would fill David in on some aspects of the story that I glossed over. I didn't want her turning my boy against me. The possibility of David spending a significant amount of time in New Zealand also wasn't one I would relish. I would miss him.

It was always likely to fail but I had one last go at trying to convince David not to go down the route of looking for Sue.

'Our kid, your mother abandoned you. Why would you want to find her?'

'Because she's my mother.'

'In what sense? Val was your mother. She was the one who changed your nappies. She was the one who never missed a school nativity play despite them all being mind-numbingly boring. She was the one who cleared up the sick off your bedroom floor when you and Graham stole my Scotch.'

'She wasn't the one who gave birth to me though, was she?'

'But she abandoned you, son,' I repeated.

'She must have had her reasons.'

I wasn't sure how far to push this one. In the end I went for a lot. 'Selfishness? Putting her career first? Revenge?'

'Revenge? You actually think she handed her baby to you just to see the look of panic on your face when Mum found out about your affair?'

'I don't know why she did what she did,' I said, 'but Val already knew about the affair. I couldn't look her in the eye without fronting up to her when she got back from Europe.'

'You surprise me.'

David didn't need to know, but Val actually heard about our affair through a busybody musician friend who saw Sue and me being over-friendly at the Pink Floyd concert. When she heard about it, Val came home and smashed ten tonnes of shite out of my best guitar. We were only just talking again by the time Sue re-entered our lives with David.

'So what happened when Sue turned up?'

'Your mother instantly got maternal. Her whole attention was focussed on you. The one question she asked me after Sue walked away from our front door was, "How do you know the baby's yours?"'

David nodded. He seemed to look me up and down. I instantly knew what he was doing.

'Don't be daft, our kid. Just look at us. We're too alike.'

'We might be alike in looks, Dad, but I'm beginning to think we're not that alike in other ways.' Fair comment. If he was in my situation, David wouldn't have done what I did, but his life would have been poorer as a result.

It was David's turn to drain the contents of his glass. My glass was already empty. I was definitely feeling the effects of the alcohol.

David moved the conversation on to what I knew about Sue. He asked about her birthday, her family, her friends, whether she released any records and the date she came into the country. Not knowing most of these details, I wasn't much help to him.

Eventually, David sat back and put his hands in his lap. With some relief, I began to sense he was running out of questions.

I was wrong, he was just shifting gears.

'Do you even know her height?'

'She was tall, but she did wear heels a lot.'

'What shoe size was she?'

'How the hell should I know? I was more interested in her bra size.'

'This isn't a fucking joke, you know.' David bolted to his feet, his chair crashing to the floor behind him. 'You must know more than you're letting on. It's obvious you loved her, for fuck's sake. I'm sick of secrets. They stop right now.'

By the end of his rant, his skin was taut, his face the colour of boiled shite. His musty breath was hot, his nose only inches from mine.

I looked away. The realisation that I would have to tell David his mother's full name depressed me immensely. My aim had been to ride this one out.

David wasn't going to allow that to happen though. He wasn't going to let this rest until he found her.

After exhaling deeply, I uttered the two words David wanted to hear. 'Sue Elsmere.'

He just looked at me. Shocked, punch-drunk. Or maybe just drunk. I couldn't tell from his expression whether he was relieved I had at last told him her name or angry that it had taken me so long.

'Why didn't you tell me that in the first place?' It was the latter then.

Ignoring his question, I gave him the other bit of information that would help him find Sue. 'She was from a town called Palmerston North.'

That was all I had. But having done some digging myself, I knew it would be enough.

Despite the knowledge that David would probably find Sue, and that our relationship would undoubtedly change as a result, I felt strangely less stressed once I had revealed his mother's full name. The cat was out of the bag. I could relax in the knowledge that I was no longer intentionally stopping my boy from finding Sue.

Whereas I was breathing easier, David looked the opposite. There was a light sheen of sweat forming on his shaven head. Again it could have been the alcohol but I doubted it. 'This isn't a game anymore, is it, son,' I said while squeezing his shoulder. He was realising his birth mother was practically only a phone call away.

'No,' our kid agreed, 'it's not a game now.'

Part Three

Dave Fazackerley

Chapter Nine

Feeling tired, preoccupied and more than a little hungover, work was the last place I wanted to be the following morning. At least it was a Friday.

No matter how hard I tried to throw myself into my job, Sue Elsmere kept forcing her way back into my thoughts. I resisted for a while, but by the mid-morning lull in foot traffic, I gave in to the inevitable. I googled Sue's full name and home town. A quick scan of the results revealed a few definite leads to follow.

Suddenly, my mother had gone from being some mythical being to having a name. She seemed a thousand times more real. It might not prove difficult to track her down, to find out her phone number and even to view a picture of her online.

That thought unnerved me. I regularly texted ex-girlfriends when I was drunk on a Friday night. There was a distinct possibility that my first contact with my birth mother for forty years would be a drunken phone call along the lines of, 'Hello, it's Dave, your son. I really luuuvvv you.'

I was jolted from my reverie by my boss. Jezz was manically clicking his fingers in front of my nose. 'Concentrate, Dave, you've got a customer.'

As my eyes drifted upwards from my phone screen,

I saw the bluest blue rinse I have ever seen peering over the counter. Until I lifted my backside from my seat, the eyes and the hair were all I could see through my window. She must have only been about four foot tall.

The old dear wanted to cash a cheque. She asked for her cash in ten pound notes. I could just about cope with that. I dealt with her request and sent her on her way, only to see her turn around at the door and shuffle back towards me at a painfully slow pace.

'What seems to be the problem?' Jezz asked from over my shoulder as the old woman put the money I had given her back on the counter. Jezz obviously hadn't trusted me to deal effectively with her request.

'I wanted my money in tens but look, he gave me this.' She held up a blue-green five pound note with the picture of the prison reform woman whose name I could never remember facing my way.

'David, I think it's time you took your break.' Jezz put his hands on my shoulders and manoeuvred me out of my seat.

He was lucky I didn't punch his lights out. Instead, I left him with the challenge of giving the old biddy eighty-five pounds, all in tenners.

The rest of my working day passed fairly uneventfully. Using an immense amount of willpower I managed to stop myself from searching for a phone number for my birth mother.

After work, Jezz bought me a few pints to make up for his overzealous management intervention. He was up for spending the whole evening in town, but I hadn't eaten and my head was spinning so I left him to it after a few rounds.

As I was walking into my cul-de-sac with a bag

of chips in one hand and my house keys in the other, Helen pulled up alongside me. She rolled down her window.

'Fancy seeing you here.'

'I live here,' I reminded her.

'I've got a bottle of red. It would go well with those chips.' Helen waved a carrier bag at me.

I hadn't thought much about Helen since our last meeting at the cemetery. Seeing her that Friday night, I should have instantly been on my guard, but my slightly inebriated state got the better of me. Instead of putting Helen off, I invited her in on the basis that anything that distracted me from researching and drunk texting my mother must be a good thing.

The house was a mess. Newspapers and magazines were strewn all over the sofa, so we settled on the floor and shared out our chips and wine.

I obviously wasn't being my normal lively self because within a few minutes of sitting down, Helen asked what was on my mind. I told her about my mother not being my mother.

Helen was gobsmacked. Once she had got over her incredulity at my revelation, she started firing off ideas on how I could find Sue. She even suggested hiring a private detective. Apparently, she used one to check whether Graham was having an affair when the two of them were splitting up. That titbit made me smile. 'Presumably your private dick didn't discover any sordid secrets,' I couldn't stop myself from asking.

'How do you know?'

'Because Graham hasn't got it in him.'

As the evening progressed and the wine bottle and chip bag lay discarded on the floor, it was Helen's turn to get a few things off her chest.

'I get bored with my life sometimes. Once my kids are home in the evening, the moment I shut the front door I know I won't see another adult until I go to work the next morning. My kids are great but a woman needs adult company from time to time.'

'Don't we all,' I chipped in.

'I miss having someone to snuggle up with. Even my fucking eldest son is getting more nookie than me. That can't be right, can it?'

Not knowing what to say to that, I put my arm around Helen's shoulder and gave her what was intended to be a reassuring squeeze. She leaned in closer in response.

Things developed quickly from that point on. Like most people, once I have had a few drinks, I find that my common sense becomes less common. My brain seems to go missing in action and unfortunately my manhood is all too willing to fill the void when it comes to making decisions.

All it took to push me over the edge was a bit of encouragement from Helen. I certainly received that.

After I had confessed to her that I missed having someone to cook for and to share the highs and lows of my day with, Helen got up onto her knees to hug me. The next thing I knew, she was astride me. The hug turned into a kiss and, before I really clocked what was going on, her hands were through my flies and touching my hardness.

Not being afraid to take the lead in the bedroom, I wasn't used to playing to someone else's tune. The suddenness of Helen's actions turned me on. Before I could respond in kind, she was pulling herself out of her own jeans and yanking her thong aside. I just had time to get my hands inside her bra before she engulfed me inside her.

It was all over in minutes. And not many minutes at that. Helen clambered off me and put her head on my shoulder. By the time our breathing had returned to normal and knickers and boxers had been replaced, my brain had returned to its post. I was already regretting my moment of weakness. My heart sank at the thought of what we had done.

Helen was a friendly, chatty woman who could be good company at times. But the case against was pretty formidable. It started with Project Lou, then there was Helen's ever so slightly intense nature and her mood swings. Also, she's Graham's ex. They have two children. And you just don't do that sort of thing. And, and, and.

It's OK to shag an ex's mate, but it isn't OK to shag a mate's ex. There is a sacred code amongst friends – thou shalt not sleep with thy mate's ex. The unofficial eleventh commandment if you like. I had let my guard slip. Idiot.

My crime was far worse than some of the Ten Commandments. I have been known to take the Lord's name in vain and I wouldn't feel too guilty if I was caught 'coveting' my neighbour's house, whatever that means. But sleeping with my mate's ex... No. Just no.

Mine and Helen's conversation was stilted at best as we did buttons, clips and zips back up. Helen talked about seeing me again. I literally ignored her. Talking is overrated in these situations. She soon got the message and left me to my brooding.

And brood I certainly did.

Chapter Ten

During the months after Mum's death, thinking about my birth mother would often become wearing. After my encounter with Helen, however, questioning my parentage was infinitely preferable to dwelling on my sex life.

According to my good friend Google, there appeared to be only one Sue Elsmere in Palmerston North, New Zealand. Her address, phone number and current whereabouts were not immediately obvious, but I did come across an interesting report in the local *Manawatu Standard* newspaper. A barmaid who went by my mother's name reportedly single-handedly separated two rival groups of youths as all hell had threatened to break loose in the Silver Fern pub in 'Palmy'. The incident took place the previous year.

The article cast Sue as a modern day heroine, gutsy and confident, not someone to be messed with. My impulsiveness obviously came from my mother. I didn't necessarily inherit her courage though.

Sue Elsmere's number might not have been dis-coverable on Google, but the Silver Fern's was. That evening, in a moment of pure spontaneity as my pie and oven chips were browning in the oven, I gave in to temptation and made the call.

After an interminably long wait, a woman answered. She muttered a curt 'hello'. Was it just the quality of the long-distance phone line that made her sound grumpy?

'Hi, is that the Silver Fern in Palmerston North?' What was I doing? A script would have been useful. I hadn't thought this through.

As luck would have it, I didn't need a script. 'Yeah it fuckin' is the Silver Fern but it's five in the fuckin' morning,' the woman declared. 'Fuck off and phone back later.' The call was promptly ended. It wasn't the line then. She was grumpy. Fuckin' grumpy.

The phone call was the wrong call. What would I have said had it not been the middle of the night and had the woman given me a chance? 'Hello, does Sue Elsmere still work there? Oh, she does. Please tell her I'm her long-lost son and I'm calling from England.' I don't think so, especially if the grumpy cow who answered the call was actually my mother.

That thought stopped me in my tracks. Had I just talked to my mother for the first time in my life?

I was about to close my phone when I noticed a text from Jay. He was instructing his fellow band members to meet him in the Raynes Park Tavern for a beer that evening. He had 'something big' to tell us.

Spending the evening with my band members didn't fill me with enthusiasm, but it was undoubtedly better than sitting on my own, brooding and playing moody music in my garage.

Once my stomach was suitably lined with pie, chips and gravy, I made my way under the railway bridge and across the road to the pub.

Jay ordered the lagers before weighing straight in with his news.

'Bren wants us to play at his wedding.'

'Boring Bren?' I asked.

'Boring Bren,' Jay confirmed. Bren was a regular in the Raynes Park Tavern, so we all kept in touch with him, even after we kicked him out of the band.

'Bloody hell, that's amazing.' I was impressed.

'I know, a gig. Cool,' Jezz proclaimed as he started tapping out the 'In the Air Tonight' beat on the edge of the sticky pub table.

'I'm amazed Boring Bren has found someone who wants to marry him,' I clarified, 'but a gig's cool too.'

Not only did Jay accept the gig on our behalf, but he also offered our services free of charge on account of Boring Bren being a long-time friend and former band member. Reluctantly, I accepted this arrangement, so long as we got a few free beers at the wedding. 'And maybe a dance with a bridesmaid,' Jezz added.

The reception was booked for the North Cheam social club. As venues go, the North Cheam social club might not be the Royal Albert Hall, but with a capacity of 300, it was a pretty decent size.

We have played at a few weddings in the past. They are slightly odd gigs. On the plus side, you are guaranteed a decent-sized audience, you get fed and watered and the punters are usually up for a party. On the downside, no one has turned up specifically to hear you, and if you aren't great, you aren't likely to get much acknowledgement at the end of each song. We all agreed that playing at Boring Bren's wedding was going to require some serious rehearsing.

'Bren wants us to be a bit more modern than we were at our Raynes Park gig,' Jay continued. He made our busking outside the station sound like a formal rock concert, but it wasn't that bit I picked up on.

'He wants us to be a bit more modern? Why doesn't he just book a more modern band then?'

'He couldn't afford one.'

We talked about what modern songs we knew. We could just about manage a bit of Oasis; maybe some Goo Goo Dolls, and if Boring Bren was really lucky, a bit of Snow Patrol or Elbow. Jay suggested 'One Day Like This'. I preferred 'Grounds for Divorce' but I was outvoted.

Midway through our animated conversation about modern music, Jezz and I noticed Jay had gone unusually quiet. He was slightly red too.

'What's up, Jay?' I asked. 'Haven't you got enough to buy the next round?'

'It's not that. It's something else I've just remembered.' He looked down at his hands.

'Spit it out, man,' Jezz demanded.

'OK,' Jay looked up, 'Bren and his fiancée have got an idea for a first dance.'

'What do they want us to play?' Jezz asked. We looked at each other. Remembering Bren's music tastes from when he had been in Life in the Faz Lane, we were sensing where this conversation was going.

Jay told us their chosen song. There was no way in a million years we would be playing Ay ay ay ay ay will always bloody love you. Whitney Houston's place in pop history might be well earned but her songs had no place on our set lists. It wasn't because I can't sing that song (I can't), we just didn't do that kind of mushy stuff, not even at a wedding. I made that point to Jay as loudly and clearly as possible. 'No.'

Jay texted Bren. Within a minute, Mr Boring offered

a second choice. '"Love is all Around", Wet Wet Wet.'

'He's taking the piss, isn't he?' Jezz was still not impressed.

Jay seemed a bit put out that we weren't prepared to sacrifice our artistic principles to please the groom. Reluctantly, he texted him back, asking him for a 'plan C'.

A few minutes later, the predictable 'Bryan Adams, "Everything I Do"' text came through.

'You need to have a word, mate,' I instructed Jay.

'Bren needs to get a life,' was Jezz's even stronger verdict.

After a lot of debate, we agreed to discuss the song list with Boring Bren and his bride-to-be over a beer the following week.

The few days leading up to the beer with the bride and groom were fairly uneventful. I did my best not to phone New Zealand. I just about managed not to get drunk and sleep with anyone's ex too.

The one thing I couldn't avoid was attending a mind-numbingly boring bank training session on the day of our wedding music beer. Jezz felt some 'intensive brainstorming' would help me fulfil my potential at the bank. My attempts to convince him that I would punch him if he made me sit through some intense bollocks seemed to fall on deaf ears. Deaf ears? Maybe that's why Jezz is such a crap drummer.

Our trainer for the day was twelve-year-old Tristan from head office. Twelve-year-old Tristan arrived at our Southwark conference suite dressed in a tailor-made Savile Row suit. Unfortunately for Tristan, the suit hadn't been tailor-made for him. It was about six sizes too big. Every time Tristan gesticulated, his jacket would slide from his shoulders and make a bid for freedom, frequently ending up dangling from his forearms.

Tristan droned on for hours. Us 'front-line staff' were told we needed to 'value add', otherwise Internet banking would steamroller over us, shit on our heads and leave us for dead. He didn't quite put it like that, but that's what he meant. He wanted us to 'bring more to the table' and do our bit to help avoid a 'paradigm shift' in the banking sector.

As far as I could work out, the idiot wanted us to flog more credit cards and insurance products. I don't know why he didn't just say that in the first place and save us all a lot of time and boredom.

I never wanted to be a salesman. If selling had been my career of choice, I would have worked in a shop or a car dealership or maybe badgered people on their doorsteps with a clipboard in hand. No amount of stupid role plays would ever make me try and sell travel insurance to Mrs Muckerjee, a regular customer who hasn't been abroad for the last twenty years. With his gambling habit, I couldn't see myself trying to flog a credit card to Mr Jacobs either. It's that sort of thing that gives bankers a bad name.

Twelve-year-old Tristan spent the afternoon telling us about his fail-safe sales techniques. I didn't really take any of it in, preferring instead to watch the clouds drift by and the rain drops trail down the windows.

The day's only saving grace was that Virginia was on the course with me. She might not be girlfriend material but she is at least someone vaguely sane I can share a joke with.

'Can I have a word with you,' she asked during the afternoon tea break. I was trying to negotiate eating a chocolate biscuit while holding an overflowing cup of tea and a handful of jammy dodgers.

'Be my guest,' I mumbled, spurting biscuit crumbs all over her blouse.

'It's sort of private.'

Oh God, not another awkward conversation. Reluctantly I followed Vee out onto the rain-sodden street and waited while she lit up a fag.

'Can I say something a bit delicate, Dave?'

I didn't want to have this conversation but I didn't see any way out of it now. I bit into my jammy biscuit and gestured for her to carry on.

'Look, I need to just get this out there. It's been bubbling up inside me for months now, so I just need to say it.'

You don't. Really you don't, I thought. I held up my now free hand to stop her right there. Vee ignored me. She didn't even pause for breath.

'I'm in love—'

'Vee, I'm sorry but the feeling's not mutual,' I jumped in quickly, cutting her off in her prime. There was no way I was going to allow my life to get even more complicated.

The poor woman blushed. 'How do you know?'

'What do you mean, how do I know?'

'How do you know what Jeremy thinks of me?'

Wait a minute. Back up the horses. Vee was in love with Jezz and not me. Well that I could certainly cope with.

The 'intensive brainstorming' was worth it after all.

Chapter Eleven

Taking the piss out of Jezz is one of my favourite sports. Vee's revelation was manna from heaven. As I discovered when I bought her a pint instead of going back to listen to more of twelve-year-old Tristan's drivel, her infatuation with the boss started at last year's Christmas party. Jezz sang a particularly sick-making karaoke version of 'Last Christmas'. To me, that performance succinctly confirmed why I was the singer in our band. To Vee, it awakened some deep-seated passion within the very core of her being.

Over our bunking-off beer, Vee asked me what Jezz thought of her. This was just too good an opportunity to miss. Jezz would live to regret sending me on that crappy training course. Instead of telling her he had christened her 'Virginia the Virgin', I opted to encourage her. 'You've got to show him how you feel. He would love a public sign of your affection. Some flowers at next week's staff meeting perhaps?'

I would have quite happily sat there all night concocting a million ways Vee could show Jezz how much she loved him in front of her fellow staff members. Unfortunately, Boring Bren was expecting my presence at the RPT, so I limited myself to just the one beer with Vee.

My mates were at the bar as I negotiated the smokers loitering in the doorway and walked into the pub.

'What are you grinning at?' Jezz asked as I took my pint from him. 'Was the training course that good?'

'Oh it had its moments.' I was doing my best not to mention Vee to Jezz, as it would undoubtedly be more fun if she unburdened herself in front of everyone at the bank.

Keeping Vee's revelation to myself would have proved difficult in normal circumstances. Luckily for me, circumstances that evening were far from normal. As soon as I saw Boring Bren's fiancée, any thoughts of Vee vanished from my mind.

Bren was engaged to a weathergirl. And when I say weathergirl I don't mean one that studies meteorology for years at some ivory tower university and appears on the radio talking about anti-cyclones. I mean the type with gorgeous skin and stunning legs who reads the weather from a script on Channel 5 while everyone goes for a piss before the film comes back on.

The weathergirl introduced herself as Chelsea. She was so gorgeous I couldn't even hold her name against her.

I could see why Bren would want to sing that he would always love her. I couldn't see why she would want to sing it back to him though. Boring Bren was about half a person overweight and had long, jet black greasy hair and a goatee. He looked like a caricature of a caricature of a ridiculous-looking short, fat bloke.

Why didn't Jay tell me Bren's fiancée was so stunning? I tried to concentrate on song lists all night but I found it hard. At one point, my mind drifted so far that I began imagining myself dancing with the weathergirl on some idyllic beach while Marti Pellow crooned away in the background.

We struggled to agree on the first dance. We dismissed Bren's corny suggestions of weather-related songs (we didn't call him Boring Bren for nothing). She obviously didn't go for him for his looks, his personality or his wit. Jezz was thinking the same. 'He must have a big dick,' he muttered as the two of us were at the bar getting a round in.

After a lot of debate, we eventually drew up a short-list that included Ed Sheeran's 'Kiss Me', 'Marry You' by Bruno Mars and, at Bren and Chelsea's insistence, 'Haven't Met You Yet' by Bublé. All the suggestions were degrees of crap, but Chelsea had taken the wind out of my sails. I didn't have the inclination to argue.

With nothing much planned for the weekend, I allowed myself a lie-in the next morning. When I eventually stirred from my slumber, I opted to spend the first few hours of my day in a leisurely manner, drinking coffee and contemplating the state of my life.

I had taken some steps towards finding my real mother, but I was shooting myself in the foot when it came to rekindling my relationship with Lou. I was drifting again, like an odd sock, spinning out of control in the tumble-drier of life, with no soul mate to keep me company.

This drifting had to end. Before I could change my mind, I phoned Lou. The librarian must have been busy polishing his bookends because Lou agreed to meet me that afternoon.

Channel 5's weather forecast, of which I was

a new fan, was predicting storms. Chelsea told me the night before that she didn't have a clue what she was talking about, so Lou and I ignored her prediction and went for a stroll along the Thames.

Our walk from Teddington Lock to Kingston, and the time in The Bishop once the storm kicked in, proved just about long enough for me to fill Lou in on the latest developments in my life. Well, some of them at least.

'He's a bastard. I can't believe he could just dump the poor woman like that,' was Lou's verdict on Dad. As we sat in the pub, looking out over the river and the occasional dog walkers braving the rain, Lou proceeded to count Sue's woes out on her fingers. 'She was new to London, she had no job, she had no friends, she was pregnant and she was only seventeen.'

'Seventeen? She was young but I don't think I said she was seventeen,' I corrected Lou. 'Dad wouldn't have slept with someone that young. He was in his mid-twenties by the time I was born.'

Lou looked away. She had pretty much captured how I was feeling about Dad and his actions. Since our late night conversation at his house, I hadn't been able to bring myself to answer his calls. His affair and his subsequent treatment of Sue might have happened more than forty years ago, but I needed time to process his story.

'Presumably you're still going to look for your mum,' Lou asked.

I nodded. There was really no doubt in my mind that I would at least try and make contact with her. She might have given me up to Dad, but she probably did it in desperation rather than because of any overriding desire to be free from me.

Lou and I ordered a mid-afternoon dinner of fish and chips, washed down with a bottle of Merlot. I smiled ruefully to myself as I realised I was making a habit of eating chips and drinking Merlot with women.

The conversation didn't exactly flow as it normally does between the two of us over lunch. Lou's spark wasn't as evident as it usually is. When it appeared, her smile seemed forced. Anxious to find out what was on Lou's mind, I honed in on what I truly hoped was the cause of her unhappiness. 'How are you getting on with the book dork?'

'Don't call him that.'

'OK then, how are you getting on with Godfrey?'

'Geoffrey.'

'That's what I said.'

Lou sighed. 'Fine, thank you.' She watched me for a while before her expression softened. 'Actually, you're right, he is a dork. He bores me stupid now.' She put her fork down and refilled her glass. 'He gets up, goes to work, comes home, eats tea, watches documentaries, goes to bed and reads a book before falling asleep and snoring all night. I haven't had sex since last Christmas.'

'He sounds like a blast,' I said, trying not to revel too openly at Lou's misfortune. And then I realised. 'We made love last Christmas.'

'Exactly.'

I beamed. To hell with not revelling too openly.

Once I had settled our bill, I asked Lou if she fancied coming back to mine for coffee.

'You know I'm not a coffee fan.'

'I know, but it's what people say, isn't it?'

'It's what people say when they want a shag.' She was smiling but she was also shaking her head. She politely declined my thinly veiled invitation. This was more than a shame. Frankly, Lou made me horny. She always has and she always will.

Instead of coming back to mine, Lou gave me a big hug, kissed me on the cheek and rushed off towards the shops, leaving me to get the train home on my own.

Staring out of the window as the train left Kingston, I should have been feeling buoyant. There was definitely still a real chemistry between me and Lou. Throughout the afternoon, neither of us missed a chance to touch the other whenever the opportunity arose. The news that Lou and the dork weren't love's young dream anymore was an added bonus that should have made my day. My year even.

But I wasn't feeling buoyant. Quite the opposite in fact. I was feeling thoroughly miserable. Just as one barrier to Lou and me getting back together was shrinking in size, I had erected another one, and a hulking great big one at that. Why had I slept with Helen? Because I was a pillock, that's why.

Helen was the last person I wanted to see when I got home, but as I turned the corner into my close, there she was, standing under an umbrella, gossiping with Deaf Doris, my nosy next-door neighbour. Still brooding, I sighed inwardly. And probably outwardly too.

'Have you had a nice lunch?' was her opening gambit. She didn't look particularly warm and friendly. I don't suppose I did either.

'What business is that of yours?'

'I saw you,' she persisted.

I didn't owe Helen an explanation, but there was probably no point in being confrontational either. My anger should have been directed at myself, not at Helen. So rather than telling her to piss off, I explained that Lou and I had met to talk about my maternal situation.

Helen and Lou did know each other from the days when Helen was still with Graham and Lou was with me. They first met at Graham and Helen's wedding. It wasn't love at first sight between them. Helen was miffed that Lou was head and shoulders the most beautiful woman there. Legs, arms and bits in between too. Lou swore Helen waved the knife at her when she was cutting the cake.

Things hadn't improved the following month, when the newlyweds hosted a dinner for their friends. Helen totally exploded at Graham for no obvious reason. As Helen's face turned tomato red and her whole body began to shake, Lou had politely suggested that she should calm down. We were genuinely fearing for her health. Lou's intervention earned her a foul-mouthed rant in response.

Back to Saturday afternoon at my house, Helen wasn't going to let me off the hook over my choice of lunch partner. 'The two of you looked very cosy together.'

That was enough for me. 'Helen, just leave it,' I began. 'You and I had sex last week but that doesn't make us an item. It doesn't mean I have to account to you for everything I do.' I managed to stop there, just on the right side of full rant mode.

After a few seconds, Helen just turned on her heel

and started walking towards her car.

'Wait,' I called after her. I felt guilty. 'I'm sorry. I didn't mean it to sound that harsh.' Helen turned around and stared at me. 'Come on, let's clear the air,' I said as I gestured for her to come in. Eventually she followed me into my kitchen.

I offered her a coffee. Not because I wanted to have sex with her but because it was the polite thing to do.

Helen declined the coffee in favour of a glass of wine. It was difficult to refuse her request, as there was an open bottle of Shiraz on the kitchen side about two feet away from where she was standing.

'Helen, this can't happen again,' I told her as I passed her a small glass.

'OK, I'll supply the next bottle,' she said.

'No, I mean us. You're Graham's ex. Mates don't date each other's exes.'

Despite me doing my best to make my feelings obvious to Helen from the moment I saw her car pull up on the drive, she looked a bit shocked. 'Oh, I see,' she mused. 'You aren't allowed to date a mate's ex, but you are allowed to rip their clothes off and make love to them? How does that logic work, then?'

Me rip her clothes off? Make love? 'We didn't make love, Helen, we had sex. Or more accurately, you had sex. I lay on the carpet thinking what the hell am I doing? It was a mistake.' I was on a roll now. My tirade reached its climax with me telling her there would be no repeat of the performance, ever.

'It's because of Lou, isn't it?' Helen asked. She had turned red and I could see tears forming in the corners of her eyes. The tears didn't stop her from emptying

104

the rest of the bottle into her wine glass, though.

'No, of course not,' I lied. Or at least partly lied. Helen's tears shamed me into adopting a more reasonable approach. I tried deploying the well-used but bollocks-sounding 'there isn't room in my life for a relationship at the moment' cliché. To say it didn't work too well would be an understatement. I ended up wearing the contents of Helen's wine glass all over my face, neck and best white shirt.

Helen's parting shot was to yell, 'You're a bastard, Dave,' as she stormed out of the front door. 'I hope you rot in hell.'

Helen didn't deserve to be treated like shit. That being said, I felt relieved to have cleared the air with her. We both knew where we stood – on our own. We were both grown adults. No one had died. Move on.

'Waste of good wine, that,' Deaf Doris called as she was watering the flowers in her porch. Nosy cow.

Chapter Twelve

With nothing else to do the following morning, and with zero chance of making any progress on Project Lou, I decided to go back to my first goal, finding my mother.

Since I'd made the impromptu phone call to New Zealand, an alternative approach had been crystallising in my mind.

I was due a week off work in the run-up to Christmas. My plan had been to decorate my bathroom that week. The decorating could wait for one more year. My bathroom had been neglected the previous year too. I'd ended up spending the whole week unsuccessfully chasing Elisa, an Australian singer who, in a short period of time, had got under my skin in a way that no one other than Lou had managed to do.

Giving myself no chance to change my mind, as soon as I had mentally made the decision to travel to New Zealand, I got on the phone to my travel agent (first name's Thomas…). My credit card took a bit of a battering, but, like most bankers, I put that worry aside for the time being.

Travelling to Palmerston North without a clear plan of attack might not have been a particularly rational decision to take, but in my experience, rational only gets you so far. The rush I felt once the confirmation email was in my inbox was all the indication I needed that I was doing the right thing.

Once my tickets were booked, updating Dad seemed an appropriate thing to do. I hadn't actively been avoiding Dad for the past few weeks, but returning his calls and texts hadn't been a priority. I blamed my hectic sex life (shagging my mate's ex and trying to sleep with my ex) for keeping me busy, but in truth, I had just needed to put a bit of space between me and my father. Dad enthusiastically accepted my invitation to lunch.

The rest of the morning tested my multi-tasking skills to their limit. In the two hours before Dad arrived, I managed to clean, tidy and cook. As he walked up my drive, the exotic aroma of home-made chicken and spinach curry would have tantalised Dad's taste buds well before the whiff of bleach commenced its assault on his nasal glands.

We had a leisurely lunch, during which we talked about nothing more significant than the weather. And maybe a weather girl. But as he was mopping up the remnants of his curry with a naan, Dad brought the subject around to more substantial matters. 'Do you hate me for what I've done?'

I watched him as he licked the sauce off his knife, a habit he must have reacquired since Mum's death as she wouldn't have tolerated such behaviour.

'I'm sure you're not proud of yourself,' I speculated, 'but you're my dad.' He had taken advantage of a young woman and then deserted her in her hour of need. I had certainly lost a bit of respect for Dad, yet I couldn't bring myself to stay angry with him. My litany of shameful moments might not have trumped Dad's exploits but it was enough to take away my right to judge.

'Thanks, our kid,' he said. He put his cutlery down and mopped his brow with the back of his hand. It could have been the spice that caused him to sweat, but I wasn't so sure.

'What's done is done,' I reassured him as I got up to clear the plates. Dad got up too and put his hands on my shoulders as if he was about to hug me, but he wasn't a natural hugger and ended up settling for a squeeze of the shoulders.

As we were loading the dishwasher, I told him about my planned trip to the other side of the world.

'What if you don't find her?' he wondered.

'What if I do?'

'What if she isn't there, or maybe she is there but she doesn't want to talk to you? What if she's got a family of her own?'

'What if she is a green scaly alien with an attitude problem? I won't know until I talk to her, will I?'

We had a jam in my garage after lunch, with Dad on Jay's guitar and me on my keyboard. It was the first time we had played together for years. When I was living at home, the two of us, or sometimes the three of us if Mum wasn't busy, would agree an artist and then work through a few of the most notable tunes in that artist's back catalogue.

I let Dad choose today. He chose Chicago, one of Mum's favourites. Not really one of mine, but I didn't grumble. 'If You Leave Me Now' and 'Hard Habit to Break' weren't too bad. When we moved on to 'Hard to Say I'm Sorry', Dad stopped playing midway through. 'I am sorry, boy,' he announced, putting Jay's guitar down. 'I'm sorry for all of this. I never set out to hurt anyone.'

As I started to pacify him, he cut me off. 'Will you apologise to Sue for me if you meet her? She won't forgive me, but just tell her, will you? I've always felt guilty.'

When I nodded my agreement, Dad surprised me by offering to pay for my trip. At first I declined, but then he became more insistent.

'You don't know how much it's costing me,' I cautioned him.

'Tell me. Flights and accommodation.'

'All in, about two thousand pounds.'

My response elicited a wry smile from Dad, but he promised to put the money in my account by the following morning.

We might have cleared the air between us, but Dad and I still weren't totally relaxed in each other's company that afternoon.

Once he headed off home, I sat down, put my feet up and fired up my laptop. My intention was to surf the net to see what else I could discover about Sue Elsmere.

My laptop was still running its opening script when the doorbell rang. Assuming it would be Dad coming back to pick up whatever he had forgotten, I headed for the door. It wasn't Dad.

'What the fuck are you playing at?' my ex-wife yelled at me.

I must have looked confused. Lou wasted no time in clarifying the situation.

'I have just been publicly humiliated by that

fucking fruitcake Helen Hopeless.'

Oh God. God, God, God, God.

'She just told me, in front of everyone else in the beans and pulses section of the supermarket, to stop ruining her love life.'

'Oh, Lou, I'm sorry,' was all I could manage in response. I needed to know how many of those beans Helen had spilled.

'So you bloody should be.'

'What did you say?' I was still fishing.

'When I told the stupid bitch I didn't know she had a love life, she took great pleasure in telling me and everyone else she was sleeping with you.'

Quite a lot of beans then. 'I'm sorry, Lou. It was a mistake. A one-off mistake.'

'So was marrying you.'

This was my worst nightmare. I knew my encounter with Helen would come back to haunt me.

Close to being lost for words, I did my best to pacify Lou. 'I was vulnerable. I needed you but you weren't there.' Even as that line came out of my mouth, I knew it sounded pathetic.

'I don't give a shit what you do, Dave, but don't ever let that bitch Helen Hopeless embarrass me in public again.' And having got that off her chest, Lou stormed back to her car and drove off, tires squealing.

'Nice to see you, Louise,' Deaf Doris chortled as she opened her front door, watering can in hand.

Fuck off, Doris.

Once I had finished banging my head against my doorframe, a couple of things occurred to me about the exchange. Firstly, Lou was angry. She rarely, if ever, got shouty angry. Maybe that meant she still cared. And secondly, Lou was right. Helen was showing alarming evidence of being a fruitcake. What right did she have to discuss our secrets with someone else? As I retreated back into my lounge, images of *Fatal Attraction* were forming in my head. At least Michael Douglas's obsessive was attractive.

It suddenly struck me that Helen might also shout her mouth off to Graham. I didn't know whether he shopped in the same supermarket as his ex, but I didn't want to take the chance. The right thing to do was to tell my best mate about our encounter myself rather than leaving it to his ex to give him the gory details.

Graham only lived a mile or so from me, off Martin Way in Morden. Having already had a few drinks with Dad over lunch, I left my car on the drive and half-walked, half-jogged across the playing fields and football pitches that lay between our two abodes.

Despite being out of breath when I got there, I was too het up to beat around the bush. We hadn't even made it through the small flat's hall when I started unburdening myself.

'Mate, I'm sorry, but I've done a really shitty thing.'

'What, forgot the beers?'

'I slept with your ex…'

'Dave…'

'I'm sorry, mate. I shagged Helen. We were drunk and she just sort of ripped her knickers off and jumped me.'

'You shagged Mum,' Sean, Graham's youngest, said, appearing in the lounge doorway. 'That's disgusting.' No wonder Graham was looking so panicky.

Instantly feeling mortified, I tried apologising

to Sean. He waved off my apology. He had more practical matters on his mind. 'You did use a condom, didn't you? I hate babies.' God, I hadn't even thought of that possibility.

As quickly as he could, Graham enticed Sean back into the lounge. I could hear the drone of some rubbishy American sitcom on the telly. I retreated to the kitchen and cracked open the beers.

When he rejoined me, Graham was understandably peeved. He seemed more perturbed by his son overhearing my confession than about the actual sex act itself. In a funny sort of way, he seemed to quite enjoy hearing my tales of woe with his ex. He could afford to be magnanimous because he was still all loved up with his new squeeze, Amy.

'God, I'm so embarrassed,' I confessed, as we both stood leaning on opposite work surfaces in Graham's small galley kitchen.

'Mate, if you want to see Helen then that's fine with me,' Graham offered, 'just don't ever start trying to be a dad to my kids.'

'I don't want to see Helen,' I clarified. 'I want Lou back.'

'Why did you sleep with Helen then?'

Good question.

Other than coming clean with Graham, my main reason for going to see him was to ask about Helen's mental state. 'She's been more persistent than I would consider healthy,' I explained. 'Wasn't there a time a while back when the police were interviewing her about that hit and run?'

Graham dismissed my fears with a shrug. 'She might be intense, but she isn't deranged. If you think she's going to stalk you, then you need to get over yourself.'

That told me then.

Chapter Thirteen

Rushing in to work after a weekend is not something I normally do, but the prospect of Vee declaring her love for Jezz during the weekly staff meeting was enough to put a spring in my step as I walked in to the branch the following Monday.

'Touch base', to give it its official name (only Jezz calls it that; others refer to it as the Monday snooze), commenced at quarter to nine sharp. Well, sharpish; the kettle took longer to boil than it usually does. We talked through who was on leave (no one), who was off sick (Ditsy Melanie – suspected sneeze), what targets we were behind on (practically all of them), tweaks to the bank's incentive scheme (yawn) and some new fraud prevention initiatives (double yawn). As we got to any other business, Vee studiously avoided my gaze. She bottled it big time.

Despite her silence in the Monday snooze, Vee did manage to make me laugh later that morning. Mr Coughlin, a perma-tanned City trader who liked to show off his wealth, decided to proposition her. As usual, Vee tried to swerve his advances, but the creep wasn't to be put off easily. 'You can see from my bank statement that I'm rather rich. Let me buy you dinner this Friday.'

'Mr Coughlin, you are right. I can see your sizeable bank balance. I can also see your wife is called Carolyn. Her phone number's here too. Would you like me to give her a ring and check our date's OK with her?' Mr Coughlin left pretty sharpish, with his orange face slightly redder than usual.

I didn't witness any overt shows of affection towards our esteemed manager over the next couple of days, but just in case I had missed something subtle, I checked with Jezz at our mid-week band practice.

'How was your day, Jezz?'

'Oh, you know, same old shit,' he replied.

'Nothing out of the ordinary happen then?' His blank look told me all I needed to know.

We experimented with a few more modern songs that night. Paolo Nutini's 'New Shoes' and Ed Sheeran's 'Give me Love' were possibilities. Much to Jay's disappointment, I drew the line at 'Price Tag'. Imitating Jessie J wasn't on my list of a million things to do before I died. I suggested some Stones, but the others weren't keen on 'Sweet Virginia' for some reason. 'I reckon that one will grow on you,' I predicted to Jezz as we packed up and headed off down the pub.

Our next practice was on a Sunday morning, just before my trip to the other side of the world. This time, Jezz did waltz into my garage with a definite spring in his step. 'Evening, ladies,' he chortled, slapping both of us on the back as he made his way to his beloved drum throne.

'Someone had a good night last night then,' Jay retorted.

'Might have.' Jezz had the smuggest of smug grins on his face.

When I once again suggested that we start off with 'Sweet Virginia', our drummer called me names.

'How the fuck do you know?' he asked, once the insults had stopped flying around.

'Everyone knew. We've known for months.'

'Known what?' Jay asked.

Despite my persistent questioning throughout the day, Jezz wouldn't confirm whether or not he was still calling her Virginia the Virgin.

My last rehearsal before New Zealand ended in the RPT with a few beers, some great banter and the traditional purchase of several packets of condoms for the newly loved-up one.

We must have had too much to drink because when the Irish guy with the red glasses started recruiting teams for the Sunday evening pub quiz, Jezz stuck his hand up. 'OK, Dennis, we'll do it.'

Neither Jezz, Jay nor I are your average Mastermind viewers. I watched it once, but that was only because the football was due on afterwards. None of us is particularly academic, and, whereas good quiz teams are made up of people specialising in different subjects, we were all experts in the same thing – 1980s pop music. Jay isn't bad on female porn stars but that subject doesn't tend to come up too often.

'Why are we doing this?' I asked as I brought the latest round of beers and condoms back to my fellow quiz team members.

'It'll be a good laugh,' Jezz assured me as he handed me the pen and paper. 'We'll know more of the answers than you, so you can write.'

My first task was to write our team name at the top

of the sheet. 'What about the Wimbledon Wankers?' Jezz asked.

'You can't use bad language in the team name, this is a family quiz,' Jay countered.

'OK, Life in the Faz Lane then? It might be good advertising.'

Jay clapped his hands together. 'Oh yeah, good idea.' Good idea my backside. I scribbled my own choice down.

Once everyone had handed their team names in, Dennis Taylor got his microphone and tin pot PA out and told us who we were up against. 'The West Wimbledon Horticultural Society,' he began, 'the Worple Road Residents' Association, the Cottenham Park Allotment Club, St Mary's Bible Group.'

'What a bunch of boring fuckers,' Jezz whispered.

'The Lords and Ladies, the Equestrian Ensemble, the Cobham Linguists,' the quizmaster droned on.

'The Cobham Linguists,' I muttered to myself.

'The Cunnilinguists,' Jezz exclaimed loudly enough to be overheard by Dennis, 'who would call themselves the Cunnilinguists?'

'The Cobham Linguists,' Dennis repeated in a stern voice. He cleared his throat before announcing the final team name, 'and Virginia's a Virgin.'

'You twat.' Jezz wasn't happy. I wasn't happy either. The Cobham Linguists?

'And the first round is on 1980s pop music,' our God-like host proclaimed. 'Question one, who had a solo hit in 1981 with "In the Air Tonight"?'

At the end of the round, quizmaster Dennis instructed everyone to swap their papers. Getting up to give our answers to the team sitting in the next booth,

I came face to face with a beard and accompanying woolly cardigan.

'What the hell are you doing on our patch?' I asked.

'Ah, The Book Thief,' the dork replied.

'Fuck you.' I strived for the intellectual high ground but probably didn't quite get there.

Annoyingly, despite the beard, the book dork was more attractive than I remembered him being. His height and girth came as a surprise to me, as did his muscles. The white T-shirt visible through his undone cardigan revealed a six-pack that put anything I had to offer to shame. There must be some heavy books in his library.

Lou's lover looked me up and down, then handed his team's answer sheet to me without further comment. He returned to his Emilys, Olivias and Bunnys. A quick scan told me that Lou wasn't with them. She obviously had more sense than to waste her Sunday night at a pub quiz. I took the opportunity to send her a quick text. 'I'm drinking with the dork.'

Lou's reply came through as we were going through the answers to round one. 'What the hell are you doing at a pub quiz?'

Miraculously, having only got one question wrong, we were in the lead at the end of round one. 'I'm very intellectually thrashing the pants off him.' Point 3 of Project Lou was going well.

The second round was on Latin American geography. The Cobham Linguists aced it, thanks, if their rowdy congratulatory remarks were anything to go by, to Geoff's encyclopaedic knowledge. 'Don't get too excited, the Cunnilinguists never come first,' Jezz cautioned them.

Funnily enough, I didn't text Lou at the end of that round. As we didn't know much about the Renaissance movement, wildlife native to Britain or the periodic table, my monthly text limit remained intact.

When we weren't floundering around trying to answer impossible questions, we spent our time inventing ways of doing the Cobham Linguists out of points. We changed their answers when they handed their sheets over to us to mark, we miscalculated their totals and we even accidentally set fire to their answer sheet. Some of our tactics worked because when the final scores were announced, the Cunnilinguists ended up finishing behind the Lords and Ladies, or the Ladyboys as Jay had publicly christened them after a few more beers.

The Lords and Ladyboys cheered raucously as their victory was confirmed. The Cobham Linguists, on the other hand, were stunned into silence.

'What's the matter,' Jezz taunted them, 'have the Cunnilinguists lost their tongues?'

'This is an outrage,' Bunny complained to Dennis. 'These twits have been cheating all night.'

'These twits have been using their phones all night,' Jezz countered, squaring up to his librarian counterpart.

'It's no wonder Virginia's a Virgin if the choice is going out with one of you uncouth idiots,' the dork responded.

Jezz and I argued for days about which one of us had punched him.

Chapter Fourteen

I hadn't told my work colleagues exactly why I was flying to New Zealand, but someone obviously had. 'Good luck, Dave, have a successful week,' Vee offered as I was sitting in the staff room eating my lunch.

'Have a safe trip. Hope the plane doesn't crash,' Jezz threw in. 'And by the way, we're having a couple of band practices while you're away. Vee's going to sing with us.'

'Isn't it lucky the woman who died wasn't your real mum,' Ditsy Melanie threw in, now back from her sneeze.

The inane comments were driving me up the wall so I sloped off half an hour early. Instead of going straight home, I picked up some flowers from outside Raynes Park station and went to see Mum.

It was dusk by the time I got to the cemetery. The sun had well and truly set, meaning that the imposing wrought-iron gates were locked. Refusing to be put off by the trivial matter of the cemetery being closed, I clambered over the railings to the side of the gate. My mates and I used to scramble over those same railings when we were kids, not normally to pay our respects to our dead relatives, but to find somewhere private to indulge in a bit of underage alcohol consumption, or if we were really lucky, underage canoodling.

It may sound stupid but even though she had been gone for a couple of months, I still had a sixth sense that Mum was looking over my shoulder as I lived my life. Would she approve of my plan to travel to New Zealand? Not knowing the answer to that question, I squatted at her graveside and mentally updated her on recent events. If Mum had known how Dad treated Sue, then surely she would at least understand what I was doing.

As I sat with Mum, I wondered how my journey would pan out. I didn't really have a clear plan of action. Having been called impulsive numerous times throughout my life, I was pretty sure that if I found Sue Elsmere, I would make myself known to her. What would her reaction be? Would she break out into a big smile and burst into tears, or would she get cross and push me away?

Having made my peace with Mum, I part-vaulted, part-stumbled back over the gates and went home via Dad's. Dad surprised me by giving me a photo album he'd put together especially for Sue. It was full of images of me through the years. There were a few baby shots, some of me in shorts, loads of holiday snaps and a multitude of sport-related pictures. I got older through the album, which also included school and college graduation photos and one or two music-related pictures.

As I turned over the last page, I came across an old snap of dad and a young woman gazing lovingly into each other's eyes, with a lake in the background.

Dad was right, Sue was beautiful. She had the sort of eyes you could stare into all night. Even though the picture had faded over time, you could clearly tell how alive, how vibrant, how, OK, hot, she had been. Looking at her face, Sue reminded me of someone, but despite racking my brain, I couldn't place the connection.

Sue and Dad looked like they were head over heels in love. That one photo once again brought home the extent of Dad's betrayal of Mum. It was obviously much more than a fling.

When I looked up from the photo, Dad was studying his shoes. 'You were tempted to run away with her, weren't you?'

'I did think about it,' he conceded. How different my life might have been if he had succumbed to that urge.

When I asked Dad what he would have done had Mum found the photo of him and Sue together, he told me he had hidden the picture in the sleeve of his Chicory Tip 'Son of my Father' single. Mum hated the song so there was no way she would have found it.

I left Dad to his own devices, or to the next-door neighbour, and went home to finish off my packing and get an early night.

Graham picked me up at the crack of dawn. Whenever either one of us went on holiday, the other would do the airport run as it saved a fortune on parking charges.

We were quiet as he negotiated his way through the west London traffic. Graham did try making conversation but my uncommunicative responses led him to give up by the time we got to the A3. I was too preoccupied with the adventure that lay ahead of me to engage in idle chitchat.

As we neared the airport, my phone brought me back into the present. It was Helen. Ignoring the call, I put the phone back into my pocket. I didn't want to talk to Helen, especially when I was sitting next to her ex.

The wretched thing continued to vibrate on and off for another few minutes. Irrational as it may sound, I had this sudden vision of the bloody woman herself jumping up and down in my pocket, demanding attention. When the vibrating eventually stopped, my breathing slowed back down and I relaxed back in my seat.

My relief was to be short-lived though. As I was wondering what Helen could possibly have wanted with me, Graham's phone sprang into life.

'It's Helen,' he announced. Oh God. Graham put the phone on speaker and said hello.

'Are you with Dave?' she asked. Shit. I frantically shook my head.

'Yes,' my best friend responded, enjoying the look of utter terror that spread across my face.

'Well, tell him I'm pregnant with his baby.'

Chapter Fifteen

As life-changing moments go, that one was up there with the best of them. I wasn't only speechless, I nearly choked on my tongue.

Luckily for me, Graham remained calm. 'What the fuck?' Well, calm-ish.

I felt as though the world had stopped and everyone in it was waiting for me to do something. Staring out at the road ahead of me, what I had just heard was beyond my comprehension.

'Dave, can you hear me?' Helen's voice broke the silence.

I still couldn't find my voice, so Graham jumped in again. 'How the hell could that have happened?'

'You should know, somehow you managed it twice yourself in your time,' she responded.

After decelerating into another traffic jam, Graham risked another comment. 'You're too old to have a baby.' He looked to me for confirmation. Coming to my senses, I may have even nodded.

'Apparently I'm not,' came the acid-coated response from the phone.

The traffic slowly started moving again. I don't know how he managed to concentrate, but Graham somehow got us into the drop-off area at Heathrow.

Helen had hung up after delivering her bombshell, leaving Graham and me alone with our respective thoughts.

'God, what the hell will the kids make of that?' my friend asked aloud. He directed his next question at me. 'What are you going to do?'

'I'm going to go to New Zealand and never come back.' At that moment, I was only half-joking.

Leaving Graham to stew over Helen's news, I went into the airport to check in. And to stew over Helen's news.

My hope as I closed my eyes as the plane took off was that I would be able to leave my problems behind me. But the sort of problems I was facing obviously had wings. They refused to be shaken off.

It takes a whole day to fly to New Zealand. That day undoubtedly felt like the longest day of my life. I spent the entirety of it fretting.

Over the Atlantic, I dreamed up all kinds of unpleasant ends for my best friend's ex. How could Helen have let this happen? How unlucky had we been? Had Helen hoped for this? The bitch. I did occasionally question my own role, but basically I spent the first leg of the journey getting angry at Helen.

During the stopover in Los Angeles, the enormity of the situation really hit me. I had played a part, albeit a fairly passive part, in creating another living soul. A beating heart. I even allowed myself to feel proud for a while. My anger soon regained control of my brain though, and by the time I had boarded the second flight, I was beating myself up for being such a prick.

Most of the flight over the Pacific was spent cursing my bad luck, cursing Lou for ever leaving me and drinking the entire plane's supply of gin. My final flight, the internal flight to Palmerston North, passed in a bit of a blur.

I hadn't slept at all on the journey. Sleep doesn't come easily to me on planes at the best of times, and those certainly weren't the best of times. I couldn't even get to sleep once I arrived at the modern, corporate-looking motel I had booked myself into. Kicking my shoes off, I lay on the bed while my mind tied itself in knots even the most imaginative sailor would have been proud of. I couldn't stop thinking about my various predicaments.

Thinking wasn't helping, though. The more I thought, the less sense things were making. I needed to talk to someone. But who could I talk to? I couldn't face talking to Graham. He would have had his own agenda, with his boys rightly being uppermost in his thoughts. I wasn't ready to talk to Lou yet, either. I wasn't sure how I ever would be. How could I possibly tell her the news?

I thought about phoning Dad but quickly dismissed the idea. I didn't need to ask him what he would have done in my circumstances. He would have tried to pay Helen to bugger off to some far-flung corner of the world with the baby. Lying on my bed that evening, I could see the attraction in Dad's methods. If I had thought it would work, I would have gladly given it a go.

In the end, rather than phoning anyone, I opted to get out of my room and have one more drink to dull my senses. The hotel bar was closed for refurbishment, so the porter directed me to the Silver Fern.

When I was organising my trip, I deliberately chose a hotel over the road from the pub my birth mother was connected with. It hadn't been my plan to just waltz in there for a drink within hours of touching down in her birth land, but after Helen's news and my resulting mental turmoil, I thought what the hell.

Just in case I bumped into my birth mother, I put the one photo I had of Sue, the one with her and Dad gazing lovingly into each other's eyes, into my jacket pocket. Without giving myself time to question my decision, I strode over the road to the pub.

After I'd spent a couple of minutes in the southern hemisphere's bright evening sunshine, it took my eyes a while to adjust to the subdued lighting inside the Silver Fern. Gradually, the dark oak furniture and the rugby-themed memorabilia adorning the walls and beams revealed itself to me. It wasn't much different to a typical British country pub. Strategically placed lamps gave it a hospitable, homely feel. Was it home to my birth mother?

Although my mind was still dominated by thoughts of impending fatherhood, I did scan the pub as I walked up to the bar. A few tables in the restaurant area were still occupied, but the place was fairly quiet. I could see four members of staff; two clearing tables, one collecting glasses and a fourth leaning on the bar, chatting to a couple of locals.

None of the staff members were my mother. One was a man mountain who wouldn't have looked out of place in the front row of the All Blacks' scrum, two barely looked old enough to have left school, and the fourth, the woman leaning on the bar, was an attractive black woman with big cheeks joined together by a broad, smiling mouth.

I was actually relieved. I just wanted to spend my evening thinking about the Helen situation. Or should I say the situation that had damaged my chances with Lou.

The barmaid finished chatting to the two men at the bar as I approached them. 'What can I get for you, honey?'

In my finest British accent, I ordered a pint of Lion Red. I had never heard of the beer before but if the two seasoned drinkers next to me were anything to go by, it was the beer of choice in the Silver Fern.

The barmaid passed me my ale. 'It's all good,' she said as I thanked her. If only.

'You're a long way from home, bro,' the nearest of the two regulars addressed me.

'Not far enough,' I mumbled as I took my first long sip.

My new companion turned to his mate and said something like, 'Hardout miserable bugger.' That was a new expression on me but its meaning was fairly clear. I probably wasn't doing a very good job of representing my country abroad.

Having suddenly lost my desire to share my problems, I drank my beer in relative silence. When only a covering of amber liquid remained at the bottom of my glass, I could feel my eyes drooping. My bed was calling. As I pushed my bar stool back away from the bar, Marty, one of my two newfound Kiwi buddies, ordered another round. 'Sue, get us three more handles when you've got a minute.'

A woman I hadn't seen before got up from a table

at the far end of the bar and gathered up some glasses. I felt my chest go tight.

Warily, I took out the photo of my mother. As Sue was illuminated by the brighter overhead lighting above the bar, I could see it was her. The eyes, the complexion and the hair, although lighter in colour than it had been, were all giveaway signs that my mother was pulling me a pint. I looked from Sue to the photo in my hand. She had aged well in the years since the photo was taken.

I stood at the bar for what seemed like an eternity waiting for my birth mother to look at me. She placed beers in front of my two native friends and then got to me. As she put my drink down, she barely glanced in my direction. Even if she had stared straight at me, she would have been doing well to recognise me.

My hand shook as I held out the photo and uttered the first words I had ever spoken to my mother.

'I think you knew my father.'

She didn't take the photo. Instead, she just stared at me.

Part Four

Sue Elsmere

Chapter Sixteen

That Sunday started ordinarily enough. My first action after showering and dressing was to sort out a lunchtime staffing crisis. Sandie went out on the town after her shift the previous night and somehow contracted flu. Donna agreed to cover but it meant paying her time and a half. In a similar vein, I then had to nag my eccentric chef, Julien, to get his fat arse into gear and put the ovens on in time for the Sunday lunch rush.

Overall, the day was entirely predictable, right up until the point when Marty, my friend and number one customer, asked for three handles instead of the usual two for him and Joe. I was in the middle of doing my weekly online banking so my head was full of figures as I placed the beers on the bar. But my preoccupation with supplier invoices and overdrafts vanished as soon as the third man spoke.

Before I even clocked his looks, I knew who he was. It was his voice that made me freeze. Although there was no hint of Liverpool in his accent, it was like listening to his father.

David has never been far from my thoughts. One of my favourite pastimes over the years has been imagining him turning up out of the blue. I didn't truly believe it would happen, though.

This very scenario, David walking unannounced into my pub, is one I have often thought about. In my dreams I would hug him, we would both burst into tears and everything would be complete.

My dreams hadn't prepared me for the shock I would feel at seeing my son, though. I was frozen to the spot, speechless.

Eventually, I managed to regain control of my faculties and, as per my dreams, enveloped David in my arms. His strength surprised me as he hugged me back. My son was handsome, one of those men who could carry the shaven-headed look off with aplomb. The set of his lips was more towards a smile than a frown, which was a good sign.

Wiping my eyes, I invited my son to join me at my corner table. He helped me shove my paperwork and laptop onto the floor.

Neither of us seemed to know what to say. As I was about to take the plunge and ask him how he had discovered my existence, I noticed Donna standing with Marty at the bar. They were staring at us. Whatever was going through their minds, it wasn't half as scandalous as the truth.

David's ale was still sitting on the bar. His eyes were looking heavy after his long flight, so rather than fetching it, I signalled for Donna to make us a pot of coffee.

David was holding a photograph. He pushed it across the table to me. Picking it up gingerly, I instantly recognised the faded picture of the two lovebirds gazing into each other's eyes.

On the day the photograph had been taken, Terry

and I were doing the tourist thing in central London. Hand in hand, we were enjoying the spring sunshine in Hyde Park. Everything was new and special to us. We had only known each other for a week or two.

There were people rowing on the Serpentine as we circled the lake. It was such a British thing to do. Still being fairly new to the country, I insisted on giving it a go.

Terry wasn't much of a rower but after a bit of goading from me, he reluctantly agreed to be my boatman for the afternoon. We spent one of the most hilarious hours of our lives making total fools of ourselves on the water. We went nowhere fast and, with the boat beginning to sink, we had to be towed back to the jetty. Neither of us could stop laughing.

Once our adventure was over, Terry fished his camera out of his bag and asked a passer-by to take our picture. It was the first time we had posed together, so, at our instruction, our photographer took a few snaps. A week or so later when we picked the developed prints up, we both fell in love with the picture.

'I've got a copy of this,' I told David. My much-thumbed copy was in my safe upstairs, alongside two other prints. David watched me studying the photo but didn't respond.

There were many weighty issues for the pair of us to discuss, but we were both struggling to grasp the nettle. Small talk wouldn't come easily either. Things like the weather, David's journey and the weekend's sports results were of no interest to either of us at our first meeting. Eventually, once Donna had brought the coffee pot and two mugs over, I took the initiative.

'When did you find out about me?'

'A few days after my mother died.' He winced as soon as the words came out of his mouth. I put my hand over his.

I poured the coffees while David found his voice. He told me about Terry's wife writing him a letter before she died, and about his dad's admission of our 'affair'.

'I suppose what I have come to find out,' he said as he fiddled with his fingers, 'is why you gave me to Dad to bring up.'

I had a sudden urge to talk about the weather or David's journey, but I could see from the look in his eyes that he needed to hear an answer to this question before he would allow himself to even begin to get to know me as a person.

Gazing up at the faded, off-white pub ceiling, I wondered how Terry had explained things to his son. If David didn't know the answer to his question, then it was pretty clear Terry had told him a crock of shit. I decided to go back to the beginning.

'Terry and I spent a few months together in 1973,' I started off. 'As far as I knew, we weren't having an affair. We were a couple who fell in love...'

'You mean you didn't know Dad was married?'

'I didn't have a clue he was married. I didn't really know anything at the time. I was only seventeen...'

'Seventeen?' David looked thoughtful. My age at the time of our affair was obviously another thing Terry hadn't shared with his son.

'Seventeen, yes,' I repeated. 'I wasn't having a great time in New Zealand. My mum was seeing a man I didn't like, and school wasn't going well, so I ran away from everything that was familiar to me to pursue my dream of becoming a famous singer.

Within days of arriving in England, before I had made any friends, I met your dad. As soon as I saw him, I knew we would get together. He had this aura about him that pulled me towards him. I fell in love. I thought he did too. It didn't occur to me that he might be married. He wasn't as young as me but he was still young. I didn't think people our age got married.'

'Didn't he wear a ring?'

'No. I wouldn't have gone near him if he had.' I gathered my thoughts before carrying on. 'When I found out I was having a baby, everything changed. Your father had a mental.'

'He what?'

'He got angry. His exact words were, "For fuck's sake, Sue, you can't be pregnant. I'm married."'

David's eyebrows shot up and he withdrew his hand from mine. I could have avoided repeating his dad's line, but however my story was told, Terry wouldn't come out of it smelling of roses. David might as well find that out upfront.

After finishing my coffee, I took up from where I had left off. David listened intently as I explained how I threw Terry out of my bedsit. I wallowed in self-pity for days on end. The enormity of my situation nearly drowned me. I was a kid, alone in a foreign country, penniless and pregnant.

David didn't say anything, so I took that as my cue to carry on. I explained how Terry had banged on my door almost daily after his initial outburst. The first few times, I refused to let him in. Eventually, though, realising the need to get my head out of the sand and make some decisions, I succumbed and opened the door.

'That meeting didn't go well,' I told my son. 'In one breath Terry apologised for deceiving me, then in the next, blow me down, he suggested I have an abortion.'

When David heard this news, his mouth dropped open. Terry didn't appear to have fronted up to his son about this vital bit of his story either. Again I wondered whether I should be showing David his dad's true nature. Watching the uncertainty develop in David's expression wasn't a comfortable experience for me. But his father certainly didn't deserve my sympathies. I made up my mind to continue being open with David, about his dad's role in proceedings at least.

I went on to explain that, being from a Catholic family, abortion wasn't an option for me. Terry once again got angry when I dismissed his suggestion. He ranted and raved, telling me his wife was coming home in a few days. He wanted 'this matter' sorted by then.

'And that's when you ran away?' David asked.

'Not before I told him to fuck off.'

'I don't blame you.'

'He told me that if anyone should fuck off, it should be me.' Despite all of this happening more than forty years ago, my fists were still clenching as I relived the emotion of it all.

David shook his head. 'What did you say to that?'

'I punched him in the nose.'

Chapter Seventeen

David puffed out his cheeks. This conversation was getting more and more difficult for him. And for me too.

The pub was emptying out. Marty and Joe were the last customers to leave. My fellow staff members were probably wondering why I wasn't helping them clear and clean tables. They would just have to keep wondering.

'Can a man not get a real drink in this pub?' David did his best to break the tension. I looked at the coffee pot without enthusiasm. What I needed more than anything at that moment was a large gin, but that was a path I couldn't afford to go down again. I got David a Scotch and myself a large glass of water.

'But none of this explains how I ended up with Mum and Dad,' he complained once his nightcap was in his hand.

'I'll get to that if you'll bear with me.' David listened attentively to my account of how I came to the decision that, if being with Terry wasn't an option, then, despite Mum's boyfriend, going back to New Zealand was the right thing to do. The right thing for me. The right thing for everyone really. I knew my mother would rant and rave at my irresponsibility but she would eventually do her best to support me.

It had been easy to get over to England without any money. All I had needed to do was smile at the right person and I was welcomed aboard a cargo ship, cleaning cabins in exchange for free passage to England. I thought about doing the same to get back home, but with my morning sickness as bad as it was, it would have been like pushing shit uphill with a shovel. People would have taken one look at my pallid colour and hangdog expression and dismissed me out of hand.

My mum didn't have any money, so she wouldn't be able to help get me home either.

Giving birth in Britain soon became my only option, but I couldn't stay in London. The thought of running into Terry made my blood run cold. Had I seen him again, I would have probably punched him again. My knuckles were still sore from the previous time.

My cousin Rae lived in Glasgow. Rae had lived in the UK for years. The two of us had never been close but I was running out of options. Thinking I could stay with Rae, one morning I got up at sparrow fart, packed my holdall and snuck onto the Glasgow train at Euston. The morning sickness was bad that day. As the train crossed the border into Scotland, I had my head in the dunny. My face was as green as the fields we were bisecting. The only consolation of spending the journey in the dunny was that the ticket inspector didn't see me.

When I found Rae's flat and rang the bell, things weren't too promising. She only had a dingy one-bedroom place. Rae was lovely, but her none-too-welcoming thug of a boyfriend was less willing to have me around. After much lobbying from Rae, he begrudgingly accepted that I would be kipping on her couch until my baby made an appearance.

'Why didn't you seek help?' David asked. 'We had a free welfare state by the 1970s, didn't we?'

'Of course you did,' I smiled, 'but I didn't trust anyone professional to be on my side.'

'Why not?'

'Partly because I was naïve. But also because Rae's mum, my Auntie Jean, had been put in an asylum and ended up killing herself after having a baby taken off her by the state. Rae had a deep fear, hatred even, of professional help. Not knowing any better myself at the time, I let Rae's views influence my decisions. I had also entered England without a passport. I had no intention of having my baby taken off me so Rae's help was the only help I could accept. And besides, she had done some nursing training so I felt safe with her.'

My story was a long one. David was leaning forward, lapping up my every word. My pace was slowing, though. I was hot and clammy and needed another break. The emotion of it all was partly to blame, as was the tightrope I was walking. Telling David the whole truth would have brought on a whole set of repercussions that I wasn't ready to face, including having to deal with Terry again.

Once I had mentally cautioned myself, I was ready to carry on.

Bringing a new baby into the world is one of the most awesome feelings a woman can experience. On that fateful day in January 1974, a big part of me was on top of the world. Immensely proud, in awe and overcome with excitement.

An even bigger part of me was in total shock, though. As I looked at the tiny fingers and toes, chubby pink cheeks and erratic mass of hair, I felt so small. Suddenly, I was expected to be a responsible mother. But with nowhere to live and no real idea how I was going to cope, I felt totally out of my depth.

Loneliness threatened to drown me too. My mum was ten thousand miles away and didn't even know I was pregnant. I didn't have a particularly great relationship with my mum but I missed her. Other than Rae, no one knew where I was, or even really cared about me.

My cousin's flat proved to be a very temporary home. When I was in labour, I joked to Rae's unpleasant boyfriend that if he had his way, I would deposit my placenta on the door mat on my way out of the front door. He didn't disagree. Despite Rae making a case for me to stay longer, her boyfriend eventually gave her an ultimatum: me or him. I couldn't be the cause of Rae's relationship splitting up so I left a few weeks after giving birth. Even that length of stay was pushing my luck.

After Rae's flat, on the recommendation of her boyfriend, I spent a couple of nights in a dirty, dilapidated squat in a rough estate to the south of Glasgow. People described it as run-down. That implied it had once been nice. I wasn't so sure it ever had been. The place was called Pollok. I remember the name because it rhymed with bollock.

Two nights was two nights too many to stay in that place. People came and went from the three-bedroom flat at all times, day and night. Like me, everyone I saw there was in some sort of desperate state. Most were drunk, some were junkies, some deranged. Some were all three. The pecking order dictated who got a bed, who got a dog-eared mattress and who, like me, got to sleep on the grimy, beer-stained carpet. Actual sleep would have been a luxury. It wasn't just the crying and feeding that kept me awake. It was the constant fights, shouting and moaning of my fellow flat mates. It was no place to be a mother. It was no place for a woman for that matter.

When I left Rae's flat, she had given me a bag of food to keep me going. Once that food ran out, I was buggered. The other waifs and strays begged and stole to get by. I couldn't bring myself to do that. I was scared, hungry, dirty, and above all, tired.

On my second night in the squat, one particular drunk, Bowfin they called him, began taking an unhealthy interest in me. No one was particularly clean in that squat but this guy's personal hygiene was so bad, you could smell his stench long before you could see him. Even the rats wouldn't go near him.

He was as mad as a meat axe too. He kept trying to touch my swollen breasts while I was feeding. I had fended him off with a few choice words and a well-placed kick the previous night, but he became more persistent. My swearing and eventual screams didn't put him off, but they did attract the attention of David, a quiet drunk who normally kept himself to himself.

David stood up for me and got a punch in the nose from my tormentor for his troubles. I have never been as scared as I was at that moment. 'You were named after that brave man who came to my rescue,' I told David.

'How come you hadn't already named me by then?' David was looking tired, but I could tell he was still keen on hearing more.

'I had, about seven times over. I just kept changing my mind.'

'I thought you had to formally register a name?'

'I didn't tell anyone official you were born, let alone what your name was.' Because of Rae's mother's experiences, the scenario of a bunch of adults I had never met crawling all over my life was something I was very anxious to avoid.

David nodded at my explanation. Continuing my story, I told my son how, for my own safety, my Scottish saviour had thrown me out of the squat. Scottish David even arranged for a lorry driver friend of his to let me cadge a ride to London in his trailer. David's tough love probably saved my life.

I had been determined not to go cap in hand to Terry, but the incident in Scotland and a couple of freezing nights crammed into my old neighbour Rebecca's Earls Court hostel room broke my resolve. My life had hit rock-bottom. I knew there was no way we could survive without help.

It took me a while to track Terry down. When I did eventually find him, he was gigging in Hammersmith. I wanted to talk to him without baby distractions. Luckily for me, Rebecca loved kids and was only too pleased to change a few nappies.

Even forty years on, I shivered as I remembered my meeting with Terry. I confronted him in the pub. Paranoid that someone would see us together, he dragged me out of the side entrance and into a dark and deserted industrial yard. For a while I actually feared for my life. Terry was so angry. He picked up a discarded brick. In hindsight I don't think he ever intended to hit me with it, but at the time he was certainly doing his best to put the fear of God into me.

David was literally on the edge of his seat. 'What happened?'

'I told your dad I needed money to get back to New Zealand. To start with, he wouldn't give me a penny. "You got pregnant," he told me, "you fucking deal with it."'

'God.'

'He eventually had a change of heart and agreed to give me five hundred pounds.'

'What made him change his mind?'

'I told him how we had been struggling. Appealed to his conscience.' I had also helped him see that paying me off was easier than hitting me over the head with a brick, and that if he didn't do either, I would find his wife and tell her everything, but there was no need for me to mention that to David.

David looked thoughtful. 'So your plan was to take me to New Zealand with you?' he asked. It was becoming increasingly obvious to me that Terry had glossed over this big chunk of the story altogether when telling David how he had come to live with his father instead of with me.

'That was my plan all along,' I confirmed. 'I couldn't see a future for me as a mother in the UK. I told myself I could face up to Mum's boyfriend if I went home, so that's what I decided to do. Terry agreed to meet me with the money two days later. But things changed the moment he saw you.'

'How?'

I explained to David that I hadn't wanted to take him with me when I went to get the money from Terry, but Rebecca wouldn't look after him because he had a fever. In the end, there had been no choice but for me to take him with me.

Terry and I met at a little café off Gloucester Road. I got there first and was feeding David when Terry walked in. He stopped in the doorway and stared. Something changed within him, I could see it in his eyes. Being a dad suddenly became real to him.

'Terry smiled as he watched me burp you,' I told David. 'Even after all that happened between us, I caught myself wondering whether there could still be a future for us as a family.'

'Did you ask him?'

'Yes. But the wheels were turning in a different direction in your dad's head.'

'How so?'

'He told me he wanted you but not me.'

David was about to speak but I held my hand up. I needed to get my next line off my chest before I exploded. 'He told me I could have the five hundred quid, but only if I gave you to him.'

David stared off into the distance as he digested my words. Eventually a light went on in his eyes. 'He bought me?'

That was one of the worst moments of my life. 'I said no at first.' Saying no had included shouting at Terry in the crowded café and storming out with a crying David in my arms.

'But at some point you must have changed your mind.' Like Jonah Lomu in his prime, David wouldn't deviate from his preferred course.

Sweat was forming on my forehead. David was right. I did end up changing my mind. I sold my son to his father, but the decision was more involved than I could explain. It wasn't just that Terry followed me out of the café and upped his offer. There were other factors involved. Despite my nigh-on overwhelming desire to gain my son's understanding, I couldn't tell him everything. Instead, I just pleaded with him to remember what I had been through.

'He upped his offer, didn't he? How much to?'

'Two thousand pounds.' I couldn't look at David.

My son sat back and folded his arms. Not knowing what to say next, I drank the rest of my water. It felt like I was having this conversation with one hand tied behind my back, but I couldn't change course now. The consequences were too awkward to bear.

Eventually, David took up the slack.

'So you took the money and dropped me off at my parents' house? And then you've lived here happily ever after since then?'

Tears were now mixing with the sweat that was running down my cheeks. Feeling myself beginning to lose control, I had one more hamstrung go at justifying my actions.

'Being a mum on my own in London was hard. Very hard. Earning a regular wage was out of the question. Other than Rebecca, who was more often drunk than sober, there was no one I could turn to for baby duties. I didn't have a pot to piss in. In the end, it came down to a choice of selling my body or selling you. I have hated myself for it ever since, but I chose to take your dad's money and go back to New Zealand.'

In response to his continued questioning, I went on to tell David how I had got back in touch with his dad. We arranged to make the exchange the following day at his house in Morden. 'Your dad left two thousand pounds in a holdall in his porch. I picked it up, rang the bell and dropped you off with your shit dad and his nice wife in a nice house in a nice area. I don't know how I managed to turn and walk away, but I did.'

David reached for a bunch of serviettes from the stack on the cutlery table next to the bar and handed them to me. I couldn't hold the tears back any longer. The floodgates opened.

As I was sitting there sobbing, the pub lights went out, leaving the two of us in almost total darkness save for the exit lighting. Had the lights gone out on my dream of being a mother to my son too?

Part Five

Dave Fazackerley

Chapter Eighteen

'Do you like rugby?' Sue asked me when I met up with her late the following morning.

Rugby isn't my sport, but I showed an appropriate amount of interest in referees' whistles and balls from different eras as Sue played tour guide. When she wasn't chatting about some rugby player called Aaron Smith, she told me about her town, Palmy as she called it. She also told me about her life since Terry. She had shared much of it with her husband, Mike.

'I met Mike at a rugby match. Mike was everything your father turned out not to be. Kind, considerate, stable. Good as gold.' Sue and Mike married and lived together until his death. He died of a heart attack a couple of years ago. They hadn't had any children. Sue told me she couldn't bring herself to go through another pregnancy, but I got the sense that she didn't think she deserved to bring another child into the world.

After the rugby museum, we went to lunch in a family-run restaurant overlooking the square. Ostrich seemed to be a popular choice amongst the other diners, so I gave it a go too. It tasted like beef.

As we were eating, Sue made my eyebrows arch when she told me she kept tabs on me as I was growing up. Every couple of years, she would pay an agency to check I was still alive and living in Morden.

'I saw you once,' she said as I was finishing off my ostrich. 'In 1990, Mike and I went on holiday to England. He was watching the cricket at Lords. He thought I was shopping in Oxford Street but instead I drove to Morden and parked up near your house. I needed to physically see you.'

'Weren't you worried Dad would recognise you?'

'He did.'

'What, he saw you?'

'He surprised me. I was watching the house I dropped you off at all those years ago, and he came out of the house next door. He saw me before I could hide behind my newspaper.'

'God, how did that meeting go?' I couldn't place 1990 in the timeline of my life. I certainly didn't remember noticing my parents panicking about the sudden appearance of Dad's former lover from New Zealand in their road.

'Your dad came around to the passenger side of my hire car, got in and told me to drive. Once I'd convinced him I wasn't there to make waves, he swallowed a chill pill. He even asked me if I fancied going for a drink.'

'Did you?'

'No, I called him a fuckwit.'

'So where was I when you saw me?'

'To get me away from his wife, Terry told me the route you took home from school. I parked up where he suggested and saw you walking home. You looked so grown up, with your long hair and confident strut. You were laughing with your mates. You looked so much like your dad.'

'Weren't you tempted to talk to me?'

'Of course I was, but I'd promised myself that, no matter how hard it was, I wouldn't make myself known to you. You already had a life and I didn't want to turn it upside down. It took all the willpower I had to stop myself from getting out of the car, though.'

Sue and I spent a lot of time together during my week in New Zealand. She had been all but a child when she came to England and met Dad. Now, she seemed confident and resourceful. Her life hadn't been without its challenges, including a battle with the demon drink since Mike's death, but she was a fighter. She had come a long way since her experiences as a young mother in the UK.

I came to realise that, with no money and no support network to fall back on, Sue hadn't really had any choice but to let Dad and Mum bring me up. Her fear of professional help had ruled out state support and there was no way she could earn money when she was looking after me. She had no way of getting back home to her mum either.

Dad, on the other hand, had made his own choices. He could have given Sue the money to take me back to New Zealand. Instead, he chose to exploit a poor seventeen-year-old girl's vulnerabilities.

Mum must have made some choices too. Talking to Sue made me wonder whether Mum had been in on the plot to buy me. Did Dad go home after seeing me in that café and elicit Mum's support for his plan to up his offer to £2000, or did he keep the whole thing under wraps in the hope that Mum's maternal instincts would immediately kick in when she saw me?

My time in New Zealand taught me a lot about Dad. If Sue had listened to him, I would never have been born. He lied to me about how I ended up living with him and Mum. And he was a scheming bastard. It was no wonder he smiled when he agreed to pay me two thousand pounds to fund my trip. He paid the same sum to Sue all those years ago to bribe her to go back to New Zealand without me.

My dad has always been my role model. To her credit, Sue told me not to turn against him despite my newly acquired knowledge. 'Neither of us is perfect,' she said as she reminded me that this saga took place more than forty years ago. I wasn't sure I would be able to forgive Dad altogether, but I promised Sue I would at least try.

On my penultimate day in the land of the long white cloud, Sue took me to Wellington, New Zealand's capital city. We spent most of the day getting to know each other, talking about the little things that make us tick as well as the big issues that have defined our lives. As we strolled through the harbour, admiring some of the biggest ships I have ever seen, I ended up telling my mother about my impending fatherhood.

'That's fantastic news,' Sue said. She knew about my desire to get back with Lou, so the excitement in her voice was tempered.

When I arrived in New Zealand, I was in total panic mode. Helen's news had totally thrown me. But during the course of the week, my anxiety levels diminished slightly. I was beginning to realise that it wasn't the thought of becoming a dad that was making me panic. Lou had talked about having children at some unidentified point in the future. Unfortunately the dork had arrived first. Being a dad to Helen's baby was something I could do, and do well.

What was putting a great big knot in my stomach was the thought of not being with Lou because of my moment of stupidity with Helen. Helen's pregnancy would, in all likelihood, be the final nail in Project Lou's coffin, if, that is, that particular coffin wasn't full of final nails already.

Sue gave me a stern lecture once I had filled her in on the situation. 'Don't you dare repeat your father's blunders. Whatever you do, you make sure you stand by that woman.'

Saying goodbye to Sue was hard. By the end of the week, we had become good friends. Before I boarded the plane that was taking me to Auckland for my onward trip home, I elicited a promise from Sue that she would come and see me in London sometime soon.

My phone chirped as I was shown to my seat on the tiny toy-like domestic plane. The stewardess instructed me to switch my device onto airplane mode. I obeyed her instruction, but not before reading a text from Graham.

'Thanks for fucking my life up.'

What now?

Chapter Nineteen

Not surprisingly in view of his text, Graham wasn't there to pick me up when my plane landed at Heathrow. I phoned him while waiting in the queue to have my passport checked. 'I'm at work, come round later,' he said before hanging up.

Mind-numbingly shattered and badly in need of my bed, I consumed large quantities of caffeine that afternoon. It kept me awake but also heightened my nerves.

As soon as I saw Graham, it was immediately obvious that something was seriously wrong. I hadn't slept in two days, yet the bags under my friend's eyes were more pronounced than those under mine. He hadn't shaved either, and Graham is normally fastidious about that sort of thing.

'What's happened?' I asked, as my mate took a beer from the obligatory four-pack I'd picked up on my way over.

'Helen has upped sticks and gone to live in Exeter.'

My immediate reaction was relief, but just as I was about to say something along the lines of 'thank God for that,' the wider implications of his words hit me. 'With your kids?'

'Yes, with the kids,' Graham confirmed. 'Because

you couldn't keep your dick in your pants, my children are now living 200 miles away.'

I felt my gut tighten. Graham lived for his two boys. He saw them regularly. Even when they were supposed to be with their mother, they would often drop in to his flat on their way home from school to hang out with their dad. Being responsible for that not happening anymore would be awful.

'Why has she gone to Exeter though?' I asked, struggling to understand this latest development.

'Apparently, because you don't give a shit about her, she feels the need to be with her parents.'

'I'm sorry, mate.'

'Is that all you can say?' Graham asked. 'Aren't you going to do something about it?'

'What can I do?' At that particular moment I couldn't think of anything within my control that would change things for the better for Graham.

'I don't know, make up with her? Stand by her? Fucking marry her if it gets her back to London with my kids.'

'Oh, come on,' I said before I could stop myself, 'I wouldn't even walk down a supermarket aisle with that woman, let alone a church one.'

'You're a twat,' my best friend responded.

We sat and drank our beers in silence. I had indeed fucked Graham's life up, as well as my own, Helen's, and Graham's boys' too for good measure. They apparently didn't want to be uprooted to Exeter either.

'Couldn't your boys live with you?' I asked, clutching at straws. As if Graham hadn't thought of that.

'This is Helen you're talking about. Hell would freeze over before she'd let the boys live with me.' Graham told me Helen had just got up the previous Saturday morning, packed the car and taken the kids to Exeter. Jack and Sean had presumed they were going there for the weekend. She hadn't told them or Graham of her intentions.

I didn't even have a second beer at Graham's. Putting my coat on, I assured him that everything would work out OK. As he was shutting the front door behind me, he told me to grow up. I knew our friendship wouldn't be the same again unless I could find some way of rectifying things. My problem was that at that moment, rectifying things seemed like a nigh-on impossible task.

There was no getting away from the fact that I needed to talk to Helen. A trip to Exeter was on the cards, but how could she be persuaded to come back to London? Would Helen demand a commitment from me in return? Would I be able to fulfil her demands? No, of course I wouldn't.

My walk back home didn't do anything to cheer me up, nor did the discovery I made when I got there. My band mates were sitting in my garage discussing what song they were going to play next.

'Ah, Dave,' Jezz called out jovially as he saw me loitering in my own garage doorway, 'just the man.'

'Just the man for what?'

'To sing "You're the One That I Want" with Vee.'

'Why would I want to sing "You're the One That I Want" with Vee?' I asked, and while I had the conch I added, 'And what the hell are you lot doing in my garage tonight?'

'Apparently, we're singing it at Bren and Chelsea's wedding,' Jay grumbled. And while he still had the conch, he added with more animation in his voice, 'And what's this I hear about you getting Helen Hope pregnant?'

I took the JD bottle from Jezz and sat on my stool. 'How do you know about that?'

'Your dad told my dad a few days ago.'

'My dad knows?' I didn't think things could get any worse but they just had. My indiscretion being public knowledge was a disaster. What if Lou had heard too?

'How was your mum?' Vee asked. 'Did you tell her she was going to be a grandmother?'

It felt like the world was closing in on me. I took a deep breath and started counting to ten. I got to two before my impatience got the better of me. 'Will you lot just piss off and leave me alone. I've had a crap day. The last thing I need right now is you arseholes talking about my private life which, it would seem, isn't very private at all. And to top it all off, you want me to sing a fucking namby pamby Grease song at a wedding. Just piss off and leave me alone.'

I walked out of my garage and was searching my pockets for my house keys when Jezz stuck his head out of the door. 'See you at work tomorrow. Don't be late.'

For much longer than a fleeting second I thought about punching him. Instead I swore at him again and slammed the door.

The soundproofing in my garage wasn't that great. As I was cleaning my teeth, I could still hear an over-enthusiastic Jezz making 'Fill My Little World' sound more like Megadeth than The Feeling. Thankfully, I was so tired that night that I drifted off to sleep before they started the next song.

Chapter Twenty

My first couple of weeks back in London were nothing short of excruciating. It might have been the run-up to Christmas but I did my best to avoid all the people I am close to. Dad phoned me but going to see him wasn't high on my list of priorities. I turned avoiding Graham into an art form and steered clear of Lou too.

The other members of Life in the Faz Lane continued to practise without me. From what I could hear through the walls, I wasn't sure it was really my band anymore. Vee appeared to be taking them in a new artistic direction. Backwards.

All in all, I wasn't exactly in the Christmas spirit. So when Jezz interrupted my tea-making in the staff room and asked me to put the work Christmas tree up, I was nonplussed.

'Can't you get Vee to do it?' I asked. 'She does it every year.'

'I know she does it every year, but I want to spruce things up a bit,' my boss replied, elbowing me to emphasise his own joke. 'And besides, it might force you to stop being such a miserable git.'

As if putting corporate-coloured baubles onto a plastic tree in front of a bunch of women eager to point out my artistic inadequacies was going to cheer me up. It didn't.

'Those lights are wonky.'

'There's a big bare patch.'

'Why are you putting a bride on the Christmas tree?'

'It's not a bride, it's an angel.' We don't call her Ditsy Melanie for nothing.

In the end, I tuned out the girls' comments and did my best to think of happier times.

Despite not having kids, Lou and I had always bought a real Christmas tree from the garden centre. We would spend a romantic festive evening dressing it, with a glass of wine in one hand and tinsel in the other. The evening would inevitably end with us undressing each other. During our first Christmas together, we made the schoolboy error of not making it upstairs before the fun started. I wouldn't recommend making love on a bed of pine needles.

'You are coming to the work Christmas party tonight, aren't you?' Jezz asked, interrupting my reverie.

'I'd rather poke my eye out with a pine needle,' I told my boss as I unceremoniously snagged the star onto the highest branch I could reach. 'Whose tree has a star and an angel on it, for fuck's sake?'

'You and I need a manager-to-employee chat.'

'Yeah, Jezz, whatever.'

'Jeremy.'

'Jeremy.' The uncertainty surrounding my future was dragging me down big time. My life was effectively in limbo. I needed to get a grip, to face up to my situation before it genuinely got the better of me.

That evening, I shut myself away in my garage

feeling sorry for myself while Jezz was busy shoving his tongue down Vee's throat at the staff Christmas party. The whole world was out partying except for me. Even Deaf Doris came home singing carols. I heard her fiddling about outside and went out to see what was going on.

'I'm a bit tipsy,' she confessed, holding up her key. 'Can you help me?'

'I'll always help a damsel in distress,' I told my neighbour as I opened her door for her. God, I was flirting with a seventy-year-old now.

Doris thanked me and was about to push her door shut when she turned around and looked at me. 'Why are you at home on your own on a night like this, David?'

'Who says I am on my own?'

'Well, aren't you?'

'Yes, I'm on my own,' I sighed.

'Well, that just won't do, will it, dear. Isn't it about time you did something about it?' She pinched my cheeks before turning on her heel, leaving me standing on her doorstep.

Doris sounded like Mum. Shape life, don't be shaped by it. What would Mum have done in my position? She would never have got herself into such a situation, but if she had, she wouldn't have let things fester. She would have taken control, worked out the best way forward and gone for it. Like she must have done when Dad first told her about me.

I didn't have a clue how I was going to take control, but there was no doubt in my mind who I needed to talk to. Before I could talk myself out of it, I phoned Helen.

Like her or loathe her, and I know which camp I was leaning towards, Helen was carrying my baby. There was no way I could resolve anything until I had talked to her.

Helen didn't answer my calls to her mobile so I got her parents' number from Graham. Her dad answered on the first ring. 'Yes,' he said, his tone instantly marking him down in my book as a miserable, conceited arse.

'Hi, my name is Dave Fazackerley,' I opened. 'I met you at Helen and Graham's wedding.'

The response took a while to come, but when it arrived, it left me in no doubt as to Helen's dad's feelings towards me. 'What the hell do you want?'

'To talk to your daughter.'

'Why should I let you talk to her? What could you possibly say that would help, you little shit?'

You little shit? My grip on the phone tightened, as did my facial muscles. Who did he think he was? 'Are you going to let me talk to her or not?'

'No.'

'Well that's really helpful, isn't it?' My powers of restraint just kept my mouth in check. Nothing would be gained if I stooped to Helen's father's level.

'Helpful? You think I should be helpful to you after what you've done to my daughter?'

'Just get Helen for me, please.'

'Fuck you.'

'Fuck you too.' Restraint is an overrated concept.

After that exchange, I was left with little choice but to travel down to Exeter in person.

Chapter Twenty-one

As I drove down the A303 along with what seemed like half the population of England, I was actually feeling less negative than I had been for weeks. I was taking some action. I wasn't quite certain what I was going to say when I got to Helen's, but at least I was doing something.

The prospect of being linked to Helen for the rest of my life was still a long way from filling me with enthusiasm, but as per Sue's advice, I wouldn't follow in Dad's footsteps. Talking about abortions and offering to buy the baby weren't on my agenda.

In reaching this view, I was putting our baby's future in Helen's hands. If Helen wanted to go through with this, then so be it. I would be a dad. My son or daughter would be a part of my life.

In some ways, having even got that far in my thinking lifted a great weight off my shoulders. I was far from happy with the fact that Lou would, in all likelihood, never entertain the idea of having me back, but at least I had started coming to terms with my predicament. My internal turmoil was now manageable as opposed to all-encompassing.

Helen's parents lived in a little cottage in Topsham, a couple of miles past Exeter. I wasn't there for a sight-seeing visit, but driving through the high street, the quaintness of the painted old cottages, tea rooms and antique shops brought a smile to my face. With its narrow streets, array of homely-looking pubs and views over the Exe Estuary, this was exactly the sort of place Lou and I would have loved to have visited for a long weekend.

I manoeuvred my car into one of the few parking spaces on the narrow one-way street outside Helen's parents' whitewashed cottage. As I put my jacket on and braved the December cold, it occurred to me that I couldn't see Helen's car parked anywhere near her parents' house. After my last phone call to Topsham, I hadn't bothered phoning again. She had better not be out.

There was only one way to find out. My knock on her parents' dark oak front door elicited muffled shouts from inside. The door was soon opened and I stood face to face with Helen's dad. He was about a foot shorter than me, the little shit. He looked very old and frail too.

'How can I help you?' he asked, obviously not recognising me by sight.

'Is Helen in?' Politeness wasn't top of my agenda that morning.

After a brief spark of recognition in the old man's eyes, his features changed almost beyond recognition. His face reddened, his lips clamped together into a harsh scowl and his eyes took on a manic appearance as he stared defiantly at me.

'What the hell are you doing here?' He took a step back inside the house and put his hand on the door, preparing to shut it in my face.

'Well, I'm not here to deliver pizza.' Having driven four hours to get to Topsham, there was no way this old man was going to stop me from seeing his daughter. I stepped forward and jammed my right foot against the door. I was about to call Helen's name when I saw her standing on the stairs. Helen's dad saw me looking and turned to his daughter.

'He's just leaving.'

'I'm not,' I said as I pushed past him and stood at the bottom of the stairs. 'We need to talk.'

Helen stood still. For a moment, she looked up the stairs, thinking presumably of retreating to the sanctuary of her bedroom. In the end, though, she turned and walked towards me.

I don't know what I was expecting, but Helen didn't show any visible signs of being pregnant. She was dressed normally in jeans and a woolly polo neck jumper. She might have been paler than normal, but it was hard to tell in the dim light of her parents' hall.

Helen removed her coat from the hook on the back of the door, kissed her father on the cheek and strode out of the front door. I dutifully followed. Without a word to me, she marched off down the road, past an old hotel and a fishmonger's, and towards the boat yard. She pushed open a door and walked in.

The Lighter Inn was a traditional pub that, in the winter at least, was populated by local seafaring folk. Sailing knick-knacks and prints took on a greater clarity as my eyes once again adjusted to dim light. A real fire provided all the heat necessary to warm the fishermen's bones after a long day at sea.

We ordered our drinks – coffee for me on account of my impending long drive home; coffee for Helen too on account of her being pregnant – and took our seats looking out over the boat yard and the Exe beyond.

'So,' Helen said by way of an opener.

'How are you?' I asked in return. Small talk was easier than the alternative.

'How am I? Well, I'm pregnant, I'm throwing up every five minutes, I'm living with my parents, my own children hate me and my car's been stolen. Other than that, I'm hunky dory.' So much for the small talk then.

'Your car got stolen? From around here?'

'Trust you to pick up on the car. Yes, my fucking car got stolen. I was actually going to take the boys back to London today to stay with Graham for a few days, but some idiot forced me to reconsider my plans.'

'Where are the boys now?' I asked, realising that I hadn't even given them a thought since arriving in Devon.

'God knows. This morning, when they discovered we wouldn't be going home after all, they went off in a huff. I haven't seen them since.'

'It must be hard for them too.' I was probably thinking more about Graham than the boys themselves, but she didn't need to know that.

'Why are you here, Dave?' Helen was obviously in a no-nonsense mood.

Rubbing my forehead in a futile attempt to rid myself of the stress that this conversation was causing, I gave her question my best shot. 'We need to talk about us and the baby.'

'I thought there was no "us".' Unlike me, Helen was sitting still, her hands on her lap. There was a look of defiance in her eyes as she stared at me.

'Look, Helen, I don't feel enough for you to spend the rest of my life with you, but I do want to do what's right for our baby.' Hearing myself say those words felt good to me; sincere.

'I'm having an abortion on Monday.'

As I sat there gazing out of the window, a couple walked past pushing a buggy. I couldn't see the baby below the layers of blankets, but it would have been there, blissfully oblivious to the harsh realities of the outside world.

Helen's pronouncement threw me. I was a bit taken aback.

Not being a particularly ideological person, I tend not to think too deeply about things that don't involve me. But I do know that killing a foetus is a big deal. If Dad had got his way, I wouldn't have been born. And what right do we have to decide to terminate a life?

These thoughts seemed to do somersaults through my mind as I sat in that dark pub in Devon. Rational internal debate proved elusive, though. The sheer enormity of the conversation sent my brain into panic mode.

Having spent an increasing amount of time over the past few weeks contemplating life as a father, I actually felt a certain amount of disappointment, but Helen hadn't exactly invited a debate on the subject. She announced her decision in a quiet voice, but a decisive, determined one. The look of defiance hadn't faltered for one second so far.

We must have sat there for a while without either of us speaking. Helen was watching me, taking my response in.

'I thought you'd be pleased,' she eventually offered.

'I don't know what I think, Helen.' By this point, rational, practical thoughts were once again beginning to take root in my consciousness. Goals such as resuming my life with Lou had started to push the rights and wrongs of abortion to one side in my mind.

'Part of me is relieved,' I eventually confessed, 'but part of me had begun to come to terms with the idea that we were having a baby.'

Helen tilted her head as if to study me from a different angle. 'Dave, you and I both know that none of this was meant to happen. You made it clear to me that the sex we had was a mistake. You were right, it was.'

'It was fun though, wasn't it?' What an idiot. Why did I say that?

'No, it was shit. I was lonely, that's why I slept with you. When the kids come home from school and I shut the front door, I'm not going to see another adult until the following day. You were just a bit of fun, a way to break the monotony of life. Oh, and a way to get back at Graham for playing happy families with his bitch, Amy.'

Helen was in rant mode. Learning my lesson quickly, I sat back and let her carry on until she ran out of steam.

'I can't believe that pathetic encounter got me pregnant. It was barely enough to get me aroused. You are an attractive man, but I've woken up now. You don't want to spend the rest of your life connected with me and I don't want to spend mine connected with you.' Helen paused for breath. She looked like a woman who was in control. For my part, despite the insults directed at me, I could feel myself beginning to relax as I listened to her.

'I also don't want to spend the next twenty years bringing up another child. I'd be a pensioner by the time he or she's old enough to leave home. My teenagers are enough for me. Who in their right mind would want to go back to sleepless nights and changing nappies? Not me.'

'Are you sure about this?'

'Yes, I'm sure.' She certainly sounded pretty sure.

'How come you haven't talked to me about your decision?' I asked. 'Surely I should have been at least a party to it?'

'You were in New Zealand chasing after your mother. I couldn't talk to you. I did talk to your dad though.'

I had known this from Jay, but that fact didn't stop me getting angry all over again. 'What the hell did you talk to Dad for?'

'I bumped into him. You weren't there and I needed someone to talk to, so I talked to your dad.'

'And I suppose Dad suggested the abortion?' I couldn't keep the annoyance out of my voice.

'Partly,' Helen confessed, 'but it wasn't as though I hadn't thought of it already.'

I sat back in my chair and blew out my cheeks. Dad and I were going to have to have words. Was he on a lifelong mission to end the Fazackerley family line?

Helen brought me back to the present. 'Dave, from the moment I told you I was pregnant, you didn't show any interest in the baby. Or in me. You haven't given me even the slightest clue that you'd want to be involved.'

'I phoned yesterday but your father fobbed me off.'

171

'You did? Well, I didn't know that. But in any case, it wouldn't have changed my decision. I'm not having an abortion to get back at you. I'm doing it because it's the right thing to do.'

I was now definitely breathing easier. It was as if, like the wood smoke from the pub's open fire, the guilt at getting Helen pregnant was dissipating into the air around me.

As Helen was talking me through what would happen at the clinic, we spotted Jack and Sean sauntering along outside the pub, studying the boats on the river.

Helen stood up and banged on the window. 'Can you take my boys back to Graham's? They don't know about the baby, so it would be good if they aren't around when I go to the clinic.'

'They don't know about the baby?'

'No. And as I'm not going to be carrying it for much longer, they never need to know, do they?'

The fewer people who knew the better, as far as I was concerned. Feeling slightly guilty that I was swanning off back to London while Helen was left with her parents, I changed the subject slightly. 'Don't you want me to come to the clinic with you?'

'What, hold my hand and play happy families? No thanks.'

Still feeling a bit numb, I nodded my agreement.

Helen, the boys and I had lunch at the pub before walking back to her parents'. The boys said their goodbyes to their mother and grandparents. They didn't seem sorry to be leaving. Judging by the angry look on Helen's dad's face as we left, I couldn't say I blamed them.

The three of us were in good spirits on the journey back to London. Graham's boys, who weren't your typical grumpy, angst-ridden teenagers, were looking forward to seeing their friends and their dad's dog again. Not their dad apparently, because that wouldn't have been cool.

Feeling like some sort of superhero, I was looking forward to seeing their dad, and especially the look on his face when I showed up with one of his boys under each arm and my cape billowing behind me, metaphorically speaking at least.

We spent most of the journey home listening to some decent sounds, or, as Sean referred to it, 'old man music'. When last travelling in the car, I had stacked the CD player full of Simple Minds albums. We were only five minutes from home when 'Alive and Kicking' started playing for the third or fourth time. I reached for the volume knob and turned it as far as it would go. Back in the day, 'Alive and Kicking' had been a bit of an anthem for our school band.

While I was drifting off down memory lane, the song's title led Sean in an altogether more contemporary direction.

'Is Mum going to keep the baby?' he shouted over the din of the car stereo.

With a sinking feeling in my stomach, I concentrated on the road ahead. We were only five minutes from Graham's Martin Way flat.

'What are you talking about, you idiot?' Jack asked his younger brother.

'Mum's pregnant.'

'Don't be stupid. She's too old.'

'She is not.'

'She is,' Jack insisted, 'and besides, you have to have sex to get pregnant. Who'd want to sleep with Mum?'

We turned into Bushey Road. Only two minutes from Graham's now. I chose to remain mute in the hope that we would arrive before the boys looked to me for any answers.

'Dave would,' Sean spluttered.

'You are joking, aren't you?' Jack looked from his brother to me.

Sean was as pleased as punch that he had known such a scandalous secret and his older brother hadn't. Jack looked anything but pleased. Peering into my mirror, I could see his top lip curling up and his nose wrinkling in disgust.

'No, I'm not joking,' Sean confirmed, 'am I, Dave?' One minute to go. When I didn't immediately reply, Sean told his brother about my admission to Graham, and also about overhearing his grandfather talking to Helen about what she was going to do about the baby.

'What exactly did Mum and Grandad say?' Jack asked.

'Grandad told Mum Dave was a bastard and she shouldn't have his baby.'

I pulled into the car park behind Graham's flat.

Jack turned away and banged his forehead theatrically against the car window.

As we were getting out of the car, Sean dropped his final bombshell. 'Mum told Grandad the baby probably wasn't Dave's anyway.'

Chapter Twenty-two

My sigh of relief once Jack and Sean were back with their dad and I was on my way home would probably have registered on the Beaufort scale. Graham offered me a lager to celebrate my day's work, but, citing tiredness rather than a desire to get away from his kids as quickly as possible, I declined his offer.

I did open a bottle once I got home, though. It wasn't exactly a celebratory beer. Helen having an abortion wasn't something to celebrate. I did, though, allow myself to think about the future in a more positive light. Maybe it was possible now to put the unfortunate episode with Helen behind me.

Sitting at my keyboard that evening, I didn't feel the need to play anything overly emotional. Instead, I rattled through 'Life on Mars', 'Changes' and 'Modern Love'. You can't beat a bit of Bowie.

My music is my one real hobby. I hadn't played much since getting back from New Zealand. Band practices took place without me. Had Jezz and Jay questioned me about it I would have denied it, but I was more than a little miffed Jezz had asked Vee to sing with the band while I was on the other side of the world. We didn't need another lead singer.

Vee didn't actually have a bad voice. It was more

Alison Moyet than Whitney Houston; more smoke-affected than sweet. Simon Cowell would have described her as your average karaoke singer. I like to think he would have put me more in the cruise ship singer bracket.

Left to Jezz and Jay, Life in the Faz Lane might play classic anthems like 'In the Air Tonight' and 'Bohemian Rhapsody', but they would then ruin the atmosphere by following them up with 'You're the One That I Want' and 'I Will Always Love You'.

It was about time the correct band pecking order was re-established. I gave the band its name, I chose my fellow band members and I was the lead singer, the musical director and the owner of the band's studio, aka my garage. It was my band.

I had an inkling that my now three fellow band members were due to hold their latest rehearsal in my garage the following lunchtime. Bren and Chelsea's wedding was less than a month away.

Jay was the first to arrive for the practice. He seemed pleased to see me. 'Are you joining us?' he asked as he took his ski jacket off and stuffed it on top of an old chest freezer that had sat unused and gathering dust since Lou had left the house.

'Are you joining me, Jay?' I got straight on the front foot. 'I'm playing some tunes that I like playing. Anyone who wants to join in is more than welcome. Anyone who wants to play any girly shit from Grease can piss off to their own garage.'

'Thank fuck for that,' my cousin responded. 'I've felt like a gooseberry for the last few weeks. It's nice to have you back.'

Jezz and Vee arrived a few minutes later. They

were slightly harder to please. 'Give Vee a chance,' Jezz pleaded. 'She's added a certain something to our practices.'

'Lung cancer?' Jay asked. I stifled a laugh as Vee obliviously tapped ash into an empty take-away coffee cup. Jezz smoked too, but a lot less than Vee.

'I'm not kicking you out of my band, Vee,' I clarified before Jezz could muster up one of his famous strops and storm out. 'In fact, I love the fact that we've got a second decent singer. It means he can stick to what he does best.' I waved my hand at Jezz. Luckily, Jezz didn't seek clarification as to whether I was referring to his JD-drinking or his drumming.

Once we had got the pecking order sorted, we had an entertaining afternoon testing out a few new songs. Vee wanted to do a Lady Gaga number but I managed to persuade her that Ellie Goulding's 'Love Me Like You Do' was more her style. The thought of Vee in a skin-tight leather outfit would have threatened a mass reappearance of the wedding breakfast.

Vee and I practised a couple of duets. We weren't a patch on Pink and Nate Ruess, but 'Just Give Me a Reason' turned out to be an option for the forthcoming gig. And just to keep Jezz on side, the last song we did before adjourning to the pub was 'In the Air Tonight'.

Jezz and Vee got pretty drunk that evening. They had finished work for Christmas. I still had a couple more days to work, but that didn't stop me at last beginning to get into the Christmas spirit. My life wasn't as bad as it had at one point looked like it was going to get. I had found my mother and she was a genuinely decent person. It didn't seem as though I was now going to be playing mothers and fathers with Graham's ex, and I had my band back.

The only thing that still required significant work was my love life.

Working on my love life after I had drunk several beers down the Raynes Park Tavern probably wasn't the best idea I have ever had, though. I didn't remember sending any texts when I got home from the pub, but when I woke up with a sore head the next morning, a message from Lou caught my eye. 'Stop it, Dave.'

Not being able to remember what it was I had tried to start, I checked through my text message history.

The conversation had started off pretty innocuously. 'I miss you.'

'You OK,' Lou had replied.

'Fancy coming over?'

'When?'

'No time like the present.'

'I'm in bed.'

'Naked?'

'Go to sleep.'

'I want u.'

'No Helen tonight then?'

'She's a bitch.'

'Tell me something I don't know.'

'I love u.'

To which my ex had replied, 'Stop it.'

Feeling relieved that the conversation hadn't been far worse, I headed off to work. With Jezz not there, the day passed fairly uneventfully. The bank was quiet; the majority of our customers seemed to have jetted off skiing or to the Caribbean for Christmas. I was taking advantage of the boss's absence and playing Angry Birds when a call came through from

Helen. I was expecting her to phone.

'How are you?' I asked. This was the day she was scheduled to have the abortion.

'You can relax now.' Her voice was flat. Cold.

'Are you OK?'

'It's done. Go back to your life.' And with that, she disconnected the call.

Chapter Twenty-three

As a child, I used to be a reluctant participant in the Christmas Eve carol service at our local church. Christmas carols were more Mum's thing than mine. As an adult, though, I have come to enjoy the event and embrace it as a chance to get into the Christmas spirit. I have even learnt to tolerate the sound of the church organ.

With Mum now gone, and my relationship with Dad strained at best, I toyed with the idea of giving the service a miss. In the end, though, I opted to keep with tradition on the basis that me going would make Mum smile if she happened to be watching from her lofty position.

The church was filling up rapidly as I walked in. Despite the heaters suspended from the ceiling working overtime, most people were still well wrapped up against the cold. Doesn't God know heat rises?

It took me a while to spot Dad. He was sitting on a pew towards the front. Debbie was there with him. As I approached them, she removed her coat, revealing the same check shirt she had been wearing the last time I saw her. Luckily for me, it was buttoned up this time. As an added bonus, she was wearing trousers.

'Hello, young man,' she sang in her annoying high-pitched voice as I took my place next to Dad. Debbie first called me 'young man' when I was about three. For some reason, her greeting hasn't kept pace with the changing times. It annoys the hell out of me but I haven't bothered telling her.

'Are you looking forward to Christmas?' she went on.

'I almost didn't recognise you with your clothes on,' I responded. Or maybe I didn't. I nodded politely and wished her season's greetings instead.

Dad was scrutinising the inner workings of the zip on his leather jacket. He didn't look up as I said hello. I know it shouldn't have, but it irked me that he was there with Debbie. Eventually he lost interest in his zip and asked me how I was doing.

'I'm OK.' I strove for a neutral tone but my response was probably a bit on the cold side, like the weather.

'I ran into Helen Hope the other day,' he offered.

'I know.' I didn't really want to have this conversation with Dad. Especially not in a church.

'Did the two of you sort the issue out?'

'Did the two of us sort the issue out,' I repeated. 'If you mean did we decide to have an abortion, then the answer's yes.' Dad just nodded matter-of-factly. On second thoughts, it wasn't Dad being at the church with Debbie that irked me. It was just Dad that irked me.

'Is that how you asked Sue to have an abortion when she was pregnant with me?' I couldn't resist asking. 'Did you tell her to "sort the issue out"?'

Dad went back to his zip. 'She told you about that then. I'm glad she didn't listen to me,' he muttered.

It was hard to hear him above the din as the church continued to fill up.

'Yes, she told me about that. And about how old she was when you took advantage of her. And how you cast her adrift as soon as Mum came home. She told me how she had me on her own, and in a foreign country. And then how you bought me off her in the same way you'd buy a car. You're a bastard, Dad.' I hadn't meant to give Dad both barrels, but his matter-of-fact way of talking about Helen's abortion flicked a switch inside me.

Just as Dad was about to respond, the minister called the congregation to order. The next three quarters of an hour was filled with the sound of bored toddlers alternately shouting and crying and half the adults enthusiastically knocking out a series of seasonal favourites. The other adults, the long-suffering spouses, were lip-synching while thinking of the pub.

The minister's final sermon urged us to place as much value on presents that you don't wrap up in cheap paper as those that you do. A boy shouted out, 'What, like a bike,' before he was hastily shushed by his mother.

'The gift of our love, the gift of our kindness, the gift of our presence and the gift of our forgiveness are the best gifts we can give this Christmas.'

Dad turned and looked at me expectantly. 'Don't hold your breath,' I told him as I picked up my coat and joined the throng of people anxious to get out of the church before the queue at the Morden Brook became too long.

The bottleneck in the church entrance gradually

subsided. As I worked my way out into the street beyond, a familiar voice broke through the din.

'Tell me something I don't know.'

Looking around, I spotted Lou sitting on the wall that separated the church's small drive from the pavement. 'You look lovely.'

'That wasn't the response I was expecting but it'll do, I suppose,' she said as she jumped off the wall. She presented her cheek and I duly obliged.

I couldn't think of what response she had been expecting, so Lou had to be content with the lovely one. It was certainly accurate enough. Even though her face was ensconced in a matching green scarf and woollen hat, the streetlight overhead illuminated her flushed pink cheeks and her full red lips. Her gorgeous smile was warm enough to banish all thoughts of the bitter weather from my mind.

'I was late arriving,' Lou explained. 'The angel of the Lord was busy giving glad tidings to you and all mankind when I got there.' In response to my blank look, she put it more bluntly. 'They were singing "While Shepherds Watched Their Flocks".'

'God, you were late.'

'Better late than never.' Lou linked her arm in mine. 'Now, are we going to go and see those Christmas lights or straight to the pub?'

The Christmas lights of Lower Morden Lane were famous in our part of London a few years ago. Most of the residents would deck their houses and gardens with illuminated versions of every conceivable Christmas symbol, and a few inconceivable ones too. People from miles around would drive or amble down the road, admiring the displays and making a donation to the local hospice while they were at it.

Lou and I grabbed some chips from the kebab shop on Grand Drive and, for the next couple of hours, pretended we were still a couple.

We ended up sharing a bottle of red in the Brook. Other than the Christmas tree and the shiny, tacky decorations adorning every wall and light fitting, the pub looked the same as it had for Mum's wake.

'Have you slept with any of your friends' other halves lately?' Lou said as we sat at the table nearest to the toilets, the only remaining space in the busy pub.

'That was the stupidest thing I have ever done.'

'What, even more stupid than sleeping with your neighbour's daughter?'

'Um, yes, even more stupid than that,' I acknowledged. Deaf Doris hadn't been impressed a while back when she had looked up while feeding her petunias to see Alison, her daughter, topless in my bedroom. Alison is my age and single but that hadn't been one of my brightest moments. Or at least leaving the curtains open hadn't been.

'I've done a lot of things I regret,' I went on. 'I regret the Helen thing, the Alison thing and whatever that woman's name at your work was, I regret that one too. I regret being oblivious to the fact that you weren't happy when we were together. Most of all, I regret the moment you ever met the book dork.'

'Did you mean what you said in your text message?' Lou changed tack. Keeping up wasn't easy.

'What did I say?'

'That you still loved me.'

'Ah, that,' I smiled as I realised what response

she had been expecting when she had hailed me at the church. 'You know I do.'

Lou studied her wine glass. 'I've moved into the spare room.'

'When? I didn't know you still had a key.' My voice was undoubtedly at a higher pitch than usual.

'Not your spare room, stupid. Geoff's.'

Catching up, I nodded. This was still progress. Lou proceeded to tell me she was fed up of sharing a room with someone who couldn't care less whether she had her expensive lingerie on or not.

Not quite knowing what I should say, I just smiled at Lou's news. She reached across the table and took my hand, the hand that was about to pick up my wine glass.

'Did you punch him, by the way?'

'No, that was definitely Jezz.'

'He said it was you.'

'I bet he told you his team beat mine in the quiz too, did he?'

'Yes, he said they thrashed you. Anyway, I don't give a shit about who won the stupid quiz, I want to talk to you about why I left you.'

'You do?' Swallowing hard, I sensed this wasn't just a casual conversation anymore. Lou hadn't wanted to discuss our marriage when we had eaten together in the Italian in Worcester Park a month or so previously. Now she was initiating the conversation.

'Let me guess,' I offered. 'You left me because I was a self-centred idiot who took you for granted. Because the most exciting thing I ever did for you was make you a cup of tea in the morning. Oh, and then there was my lack of ambition.'

'There was that,' Lou agreed, 'but there's something else too.'

'The book dork? What did you see in him anyway?'

'He was everything you weren't. Intelligent, fit, attentive.'

'Thanks.'

'My pleasure. He just turned up at the right time. Or the wrong time, I'm not sure. It wasn't really about him. Partly at least, I left you because I wanted children and I couldn't have them with you.'

This was news to me. 'Why couldn't you have them with me? I'd have been a good dad.'

Lou sighed. 'You would have been a good dad, but that's not the point. Whenever I tried talking to you about children, you would go quiet. At a push, you'd admit to wanting them but at some unspecified point in the future that never seemed to come.'

Lou was probably right. When we were together, I had been content with our lives. We were, as far as I was concerned, living the dream. Having children might have changed things, although I don't remember ever making a conscious decision not to have them.

'You could have tried harder to talk about it. You could have convinced me.'

'I didn't need to talk about it. I took matters into my own hands and stopped taking the pill. For the last eighteen months we were together, I tried but I didn't get pregnant.'

Not now knowing where this conversation was going, I opted to sip my wine and let Lou continue. Eventually she did. 'I left you because I didn't think you could give me a child.'

'I could have done,' I responded with conviction.

Lou's cheeks were getting blotchy, a sure sign that tears would follow. I sighed and stroked her hand. 'Lou, this is bollocks. Why didn't you talk to me about it at the time?'

'Because you weren't interested. Because you were an idiot. Because I was an idiot. But most of all because I was petrified that it was me who couldn't conceive. I needed to prove to myself that it wasn't.'

'Normal people would go to a doctor, not run off with someone else.' An emotional battle had erupted in my head. At that point, concern for Lou was just winning out over indignation but it was a close fight.

'Dave, I'm sorry.' Lou was making a big effort to keep herself together. She resisted my attempt to give her a hug, putting her arms on my shoulders and keeping me at a distance. 'I can't have children.'

'Have you received a medical opinion this time, or are you basing this judgement on the fact that you haven't been able to have children with the book nerd either?' Anger was fighting back.

'I hardly ever have sex with the book nerd, remember.' Lou took a few deep breaths before continuing. 'I've seen the professionals. I've done the tests. It's unlikely I'll ever conceive.'

I didn't know what to say. It seemed as though Lou had just wasted the last couple of years of our lives because she hadn't felt able to talk to me about her fears. Not trusting myself to speak, I contented myself with drinking the rest of my glass of Rioja.

'There's something else,' Lou offered, as I put my glass down. I just looked at her. 'I went to see your mum last year.'

'And?'

'You know I used to be close to her before our split. I didn't know who else to turn to, so I talked to her about my situation.'

'And did she listen?'

'She got a few digs in at first about you being better off without me, but once I'd told her my story, she soon stopped treating me like the pantomime villain.

'Your mum told me you were still in love with me. She told me to do the tests. She told me to talk to you, but I just couldn't. I didn't want to be told that I couldn't do the one thing that should come naturally to a woman.'

Lou's story would have struck a chord with Mum. Neither of them could conceive naturally. Mum had agreed to go to extraordinary lengths to acquire a child. Lou had been after a similar goal, albeit she had gone about achieving it in a different way.

It would have struck a chord with Dad too. He would have advocated buying Helen's baby for sure. How would Lou react to the news of Helen having been pregnant with our child? She would surely find out at some point. I knew I should be the one to tell her, but before I could muster up enough courage, Lou had resumed control of the conversation.

'Your mum told me about you.'

'What do you mean she told you about me?'

'That she wasn't your natural mother.'

I was learning a lot that Christmas Eve. 'When did you know? Why didn't you tell me?'

'She swore me to secrecy. She told me about her wanting children and not being able to have them. She told me about your dad's affair and about how his other woman had asked the two of them to bring you up.'

'I can't believe you didn't tell me.'

'Your mum was a caring woman. She told me how she had felt completely torn, taking on someone else's child. She was concerned for your actual mother. Your dad hadn't told her much about the woman, but your mum worried about what must have gone on in her mind to cause her to give up a baby.'

If there was background noise in the pub, and on Christmas Eve there certainly would have been, then I was oblivious to it. I sat there absorbing Lou's words with total concentration.

'After living with her guilt for a while, your mum couldn't stand it any longer. She decided she had to know what drove your dad's other woman to leave you with them.'

Over the course of the remainder of the bottle of wine, Lou told me how Mum had managed to find out a bit about Sue. Having heard Sue's accent on the day she had met her, Mum knew she was from New Zealand. Once she had identified a few leads via some of Dad's more malleable music acquaintances, she had commissioned some help in Sue's native country to track her down.

'Did she find her?' I asked as Lou was sipping her drink.

Lou nodded. I didn't know what to make of this turn of events. Sue hadn't mentioned any contact with Mum. Knowing Mum, though, Lou's story rang true. I had always struggled with Mum's role in taking me on. She would have worried about what became of my birth mother.

'Your mum didn't get in touch with Sue, though,' Lou clarified.

'Why not?'

'Because that wasn't all she discovered.'

Lou was sitting less still now. Her fingers were moving up and down the stem of her wine glass and even her eyes were flitting about. Requiring an increasing amount of prompting, her narrative was slowing down too.

'What did she discover?'

'Sue had a daughter. Dave, in all likelihood, you've got a twin sister.'

Chapter Twenty-four

Surprising as it may seem, I hadn't made any plans for how I would spend my Christmas Day. Dad had invited me to his place. Graham had also suggested that I drop in to Amy's for a drink in the evening. Neither offer had filled me with enthusiasm. Quite frankly, the thought of seeing Graham's kids again brought me out in a cold sweat.

Prior to Christmas Eve, spending Christmas Day with Jay, Boring Bren and whoever else happened to be down the pub had been my most likely option. Luckily, my conversation with Lou changed things. The two of us had a lot to talk about so we spent the day together.

Lou left the dork to his books and drove over to mine at the crack of dawn. As we often did when we were a married couple, we made our way to Richmond Park. With only a few deer for company, we sat on a gnarled old log, huddled together in our thick coats and scarves and watched the sun rise. The weather was perfect for the occasion. The sky was crystal clear and the only mist came as our warm breath merged with the winter air around us.

Once the sun was beginning to attack the frost, we walked through the park, out of Petersham Gate and down to the river. While we were walking, Lou took up from where she had left off the previous evening.

'Your mum felt a sort of relief when she found out about Sue's daughter.'

'Why?'

'Because it meant Sue hadn't lost everything when she gave you up.' Mum apparently believed that Sue and Dad had concocted some sort of a deal. Each parent would keep one twin.

'Presumably she confronted Dad about it,' I speculated.

'No, she didn't. She told me she couldn't bear to hear any more lies from your father about the whole affair.' I nodded, knowing all too well how Mum had felt.

'Because Sue kept her daughter,' Lou continued, 'your mum stopped feeling sorry for her. She stopped keeping tabs on Sue and never mentioned her discovery to your dad.'

This sister development seemed totally surreal to me. Quite frankly, having already discovered the unreliability of Dad's account, hearing that Sue's word couldn't be taken at face value either left me thoroughly depressed by the whole situation. Would I ever know what had really happened back then?

So I now had a sibling. Why hadn't Sue told me about her? Could I be bothered to find her as well? At that precise moment, walking back through Richmond Park and watching the deer searching for food, I couldn't help but envy their uncomplicated existence. They didn't seem to have any stresses about their parentage.

While my family saga was depressing, what was definitely not depressing was spending Christmas Day with Lou. Because I hadn't planned to cook a Christmas dinner, while the rest of the country was eating turkey, Lou and I made do with pork chops, roast potatoes and a few limp vegetables for our festive lunch. There wasn't a sprout in sight.

Back in the day, Mum and Dad used to invite us to theirs for Christmas lunch, along with Graham's parents and, for a few years at least, Graham and Helen. We would eat vast amounts of turkey and trimmings and drink too much ale. After lunch, the men would go off into one part of the house and pretend to be rock stars or sing rude songs. The women would be altogether more refined, sipping wine and watching the Queen's speech on the BBC.

When Graham and Helen became parents, the dynamic changed. Graham would get told off for singing rude songs, we would all get dirty looks for drinking too much and Mum and Lou would spend the whole time bitching about Helen.

I couldn't remember a year when Lou and I had spent the whole of Christmas Day on our own.

Our pork lunch was good enough for us. After I cleared the dishes away, we sat cosily together on the sofa and watched When Harry Met Sally. It goes without saying that I would have loved to take Lou to bed but somehow it just felt more right to be together with our clothes on. It was almost as if sex might have cheapened the moment.

We didn't open a bottle of wine either, possibly for the same reason. It felt like we were road testing each other. Could we still be happy spending long hours together in each other's company, or had our lives moved on too much?

Just after Meg Ryan faked her orgasm, Lou propped her chin up on her hand and studied my face. 'So if you had your way, David, where would we be in ten years' time?' She called me David. I can't recall her calling me David before, except at our wedding and then again a few years later when I told her I had won a homing pigeon in a bet. Thankfully the pigeon got lost en route and never showed up.

In normal circumstances, I might have answered such a question with a glib response involving some form of debauchery. But these weren't normal circumstances. We were being reflective.

'We'd be together, with our kids. They'd be playing football in the garden. You'd be baking an apple pie and I'd be putting the finishing touches to the best tree house you've ever seen.' A bit clichéd perhaps, but not bad off the cuff.

'I can't have kids.'

'We'll adopt some then.'

'I've never baked an apple pie.'

'We'll adopt one of those too.'

'And you've never built a tree house.'

'Stop being picky.'

'Sorry,' Lou said as she let her head rest back on my chest.

When the film finished, we talked about going to the pub, but neither of us seemed to want to share our day with anyone else. In the end, we opted for mugs of tea and Christmas telly.

There was some big saga unfolding in EastEnders. Lou vaguely followed it, but I was somewhere else altogether. As the drums kicked in at the end of the dramatic Christmas episode, I dropped my own bombshell. 'Helen was pregnant.'

I had agonised over whether or not to tell Lou my news. Concluding that it was only right to be honest, and that she was likely to find out at some point anyway, I ended up spilling the beans.

Lou didn't visibly react at first. She continued to stare at the telly. The next programme had started by the time she spoke again. 'Was?'

'She had an abortion.'

More silence followed. Lou was still lying with her head on my chest, but her breathing felt less rhythmic. She shuddered and eventually sat up.

'It might not have been my baby.' I felt the need to justify myself.

'Did you ask her to have an abortion?'

'It was her decision, Lou. She made it before I went to see her.'

'God, what a mess. Why did you have to sleep with her?'

'I don't know.' Because I was a prat.

My confession brought our companionable Christmas Day to an end. Lou made her excuses in a subdued tone and left me to watch Morecambe and Wise on my own. I hadn't expected anything else really, but I was playing the long game. My secret wasn't weighing me down anymore.

Having seen this particular Christmas special several times before, once Lou had left, I reverted to type and walked to the pub. Jay was indeed there. I spent the rest of the evening filling him in on some of the more sordid developments in my family saga. He particularly enjoyed hearing how Dad had bought me from Sue for two thousand quid.

'So let me get this straight,' he said while trying not to chuckle too much, 'you're worth less than my guitar?'

Part Six

Dave Fazackerley

Chapter Twenty-five

At first I thought the sound of Fleetwood Mac's 'The Chain' bass riff was part of my dreams. It wasn't. It was my latest phone ringtone. Receiving a call in the early hours is never a good thing. The call that drew me from my slumber that Christmas night was no exception. It was Jezz.

'What the hell are you calling me in the middle of the night for?'

The voice on the other end of the line sounded flat. It didn't sound like Jezz's voice, but the words the caller uttered were unmistakable. 'There's been a fire.'

My eyes snapped fully open. 'Where? At Jezz's?'

'This is Jezz. The fire's next door. Your dad was there.'

I grabbed my jeans and struggled to put them on with one hand while clutching the phone to my ear with the other. All I could hear was coughing.

I was down the stairs and out of the front door, car keys in hand, by the time Jezz managed to get his breathing under control enough to string another sentence together. 'He's out of the house.'

'I'm on my way.' Lewis Hamilton couldn't have driven any faster through the side roads of Raynes

Park than I did that night. The blues, greens and reds of suburbia's Christmas lights were a blur as I took a right, then a left, then another left into Monkleigh Road. Luckily for me, no one else had reason to be out at that time of night. The roads were deserted.

Even before I turned right into Leamington Avenue, I could see the flashing blue lights reflecting in the windows of the houses opposite. I left my car on the corner of my parents' road. An emergency response vehicle had blocked the junction.

As I ran towards Dad's house, the full extent of the drama was revealed to me in a vivid kaleidoscope of colours. Two red fire engines, more blue lights. Yellow-helmeted professionals running left, right and centre, huge dancing flames, black smoke competing for supremacy with the orange from the street lights.

The extraordinary heat hit me full in the face as I dodged groups of dressing-gown and coat-clad residents and made my way towards the action. The scene began to blur as the smoke got into my eyes. And then I felt it in my lungs too. Breathing became physically painful within seconds.

Two powerful hands on my chest put a halt to my advance. I needed to get to Dad.

'Sir, you can't go any closer. It's too dangerous.' The fireman spoke loudly so as to be heard above the crackling, the shouting and hum of the hoses. His huge frame ruled out any argument.

'My dad was in that house. Where is he?'

Instead of answering my question, he placed his mask back over his face, put one strong forearm behind my back and guided me to the other side of the road and away from the fire.

As I walked, I looked back over my shoulder, anxious to know what was happening. People on ladders were directing hoses through openings where windows had once been. Spray and steam, mixed with thick, billowing smoke, drifted upwards in the cold night air.

The inferno seemed to be centred on Debbie's house. The roof looked like it was made of fire. Flames had spread to the left, to Jezz's roof and to the right too, to the eaves of my parents' house. Smoke was escaping from Dad's bedroom window.

As we walked away from the fire, in the opposite direction from where I had left my car, I noticed the two ambulances for the first time. One had its back doors open, the other was just moving off towards Ashridge Way, lights flashing.

'Who's in there?' I asked, pointing to the moving emergency vehicle.

The fireman removed his mask and looked around. 'I'm not sure, but this man will know.' He gestured towards a paramedic who was standing by an open car door, talking to someone inside the vehicle. Approaching the car, I got a clear view of who was sitting in the back.

'Where's my dad?'

Removing his mask, Jezz managed to whisper, 'He's OK,' before another coughing fit forced him back to the oxygen.

'Mr Fazackerley? Your father's been taken to St George's.'

The paramedic had walked around the car to address me. I turned to face him. He was young, and considerably shorter than me.

'If he's OK, why have they taken him to hospital?'

'He's got a few minor burns and has suffered a fair bit of smoke inhalation. We think he's going to be fine, though.'

'You think he's going to be fine?' I needed more convincing. The paramedic didn't look old enough to smoke, let alone to treat smoke inhalation.

'Vee saved him,' Jezz managed to say between gasps for air.

'Vee? Where's Vee?' It hadn't even occurred to me that Vee might have been there.

'She's already been taken to hospital,' the paramedic chipped in. Something didn't feel right. Despite his reassurances, the prepubescent medical man looked as though he was going to burst into tears at any minute. His bottom lip was quivering.

'I'm afraid your mother wasn't so lucky,' he continued.

'My mother?'

'Yes, the neighbours were—'

'My mother died months ago,' I interrupted him. Feeling confused, I looked from the paramedic to Jezz.

Jezz removed his mask. 'Debbie,' he whispered. And then I understood.

While the majority of the population was enjoying a leisurely Boxing Day breakfast, trying to piece together their children's Christmas presents or rushing to secure bargains in the sales, I spent the day at St George's hospital, Tooting, trying to piece together what had happened the night before.

Jezz was the least affected of those caught up in the fire. Within a few hours, he had discarded his oxygen mask and was able to tell me what had happened.

He and Vee had spent Christmas Day together. Jezz drank a whole bottle of JD during the course of the day, before passing out in bed. Had Vee not been alert to the sound of the smoke alarm, the poisonous fumes would in all likelihood have done for them both.

The two of them went into the street to see what was going on. The one useful thing Jezz did before doubling up and emptying the contents of his stomach onto the pavement was use his shoulder to smash Debbie's front door lock. He was mortified at not being of any use thereafter.

Vee braved the wall of heat and smoke to discover Dad gasping for breath on the floor at the bottom of the stairs. The bannister was alight, but somehow Vee managed to guide Dad out of the house.

Despite the fire quickly spreading down the stairs, Vee then went back into the house to try and reach Debbie. She got halfway up the stairs before a lack of oxygen forced her back.

Vee was pretty badly affected by the smoke. Along with Dad, she had been tested for carbon monoxide inhalation. They both had chest X-rays too. Nurses continually seemed to be administering blood tests. Jezz and I watched through a window as Vee's drip was changed. She had a tube down her throat to keep her airway clear.

'It was like breathing under water,' Jezz said, shaking his head. 'I don't know how she did it.'

'We've got a lot to thank her for.' I shuddered at the thought of what might have been, had it not been for Vee's bravery.

Thankfully for me, Dad's injuries weren't too serious. He had a second-degree burn on the sole of his left foot, and burns on the fingers of his left hand where he had got too close to the burning bannister. The skin on his face and scalp had a bluish tinge to it. The doctors were monitoring his cough and his breathing, but they didn't seem unduly worried.

Tears streamed from Dad's already raw eyes as he told me he had been unable to rouse Debbie. The poisonous smoke had killed her as she slept.

I sat with Dad for a while, but made myself scarce when Debbie's two grown-up daughters arrived to talk to him about the fire that had killed their mother. Did they even know Dad was sleeping with their mother?

That evening, I left the hospital feeling shocked, saddened and completely drained. But, from a selfish perspective, there was relief there too. Dad was OK.

Having been discharged already, Jezz left the hospital with me. I offered to drop him off at his house on my way home, but any thoughts he had of staying there vanished as soon as we came within sight of Leamington Avenue.

The bricks to the side of Jezz's house that bordered Debbie's were charred black. The fire crews had smashed the lounge window and doused the party walls with water. Even standing back behind the fire service tape that prevented closer inspection of the interior of the house, we could see Jezz's lounge was covered in a combination of soot and water. The thick grey sludge coated furniture, walls and doors. Everything in the lounge looked shades of grey, including the little Christmas tree leaning precariously against a book case in the corner.

The bedroom window was shattered too, indicating that the lounge wasn't the only room to have been given the water treatment.

Leaving Jezz to study his house alone, I walked past the burnt-out shell that had been Debbie's family home for the most part of forty years. Wisps of smoke were still escaping from the gaping holes in the roof structure and rising into the equally grey sky beyond. My skin ran cold at the thought of what could have happened to Dad had Vee not saved him.

Poor Debbie.

Dad's house, the other side of Debbie's, was in a similar state to Jezz's. Standing on the pavement outside, I could see the grey coating of soot clinging to Dad's bedroom ceiling. Even forgetting about Dad's foot injury and his likely mobility challenges over the coming weeks, there was no way he would be able to live at home for the foreseeable future. Mum's former home would never be the same again.

Jezz gratefully accepted my offer of a room for the night. My house is a three-bedroom end of terrace. I had a feeling that I would need to clear out the third bedroom too in the coming days.

Despite being totally knackered, I offered Jezz a nightcap before we retired for the night. It had been a stressful day. Jezz opted for fruit juice rather than Scotch, reasoning that it would be better for his throat. Once our glasses were full, I raised mine. 'To Vee,' I said, taking a large sip of warming whisky.

Jezz raised his own glass. 'To Debbie. Rest in peace, old girl.'

Chapter Twenty-six

'I can't work out what smells worse, the piss or the bleach.'

Dad wasn't happy in hospital. He shared his section of the ward with an elderly man with pleurisy and an even older man who, when he remembered to breathe, made a big song and dance about it. 'It's a fucking cacophony of coughing,' he said, before going into spasms himself.

'All you need is one more patient and they'll call this the four coughs ward.' My attempt to cheer Dad up did at least raise a smile.

Two days after the fire, I was with Dad when his consultant paid him a visit.

'How are you feeling this morning, Mr Fazackerley?'

'Sick of this place.' He was trying desperately not to hack in front of the doctor.

'Well, you're making good progress. Another few days and we'll have you out of here.' And at that, the doctor strode off to see his next patient.

'Another few days? I'll go mad.'

'You know you can't go home, anyway,' I told him for the hundredth time. 'Your house is a disaster zone.'

'I'm not sure I could sleep there even if the house was OK,' Dad responded. 'Every time I close my eyes, I see Debbie's face. And the flames.' The impact of the fire on Dad's mental state would be longer lasting than any physical impact he suffered.

I had called in at Dad's on my way to the hospital that morning, partly to talk to someone from the fire service and partly just to satisfy my curiosity.

The downstairs was a total mess, but mostly only a cosmetic mess. The upstairs, though, had suffered big time. Part of the ceiling in his en suite had caved in and the walls in his bedroom were charred. To my untrained eye, it looked as though a lot of the plaster upstairs would need replacing. The house was a serious insurance job.

Dad sighed noisily. His breathing was much better by then, but it was a still a million miles from returning to normal. He was taking short, shallow breaths. Talking in long sentences remained hard work for him too.

'Did they say what caused the fire?'

'They couldn't be certain exactly what caused it, but they think it started on the landing,' I told Dad. 'There was an electric heater there, apparently.'

Rubbing his eyes with his good hand, Dad seemed to shrink back into himself. A tear rolled down his cheek. 'I was supposed to turn it off before going to bed,' he said.

'It was probably a faulty plug or something,' I offered without much sincerity. 'You couldn't have foreseen that happening.'

Dad shook his head. He leant back on his pillow

and looked up at the fluorescent lights above his bed. 'I kept nagging her about a smoke alarm too. I should have sorted it myself.'

'It's not your fault, Dad,' I repeated because it seemed the right thing to say.

'I loved her, you know.'

Dad and I hadn't talked much about Debbie, but I had already seen it in his eyes. A light seemed to have gone out in a way that it hadn't necessarily done when Mum had died.

'How long were you seeing her for, Dad?'

'You don't want to know.'

'You like deciding what I do and don't want to know, don't you?' Even with the fire, it didn't take much for my anger at Dad to resurface.

If he had kept his mouth shut and continued to stare at the ceiling, I would probably have calmed down pretty quickly, but instead Dad chose that moment to open up. 'A few years. Your mother'd go to her dance club, I'd go next door.'

He was right, I didn't want to know. The realisation that Dad had been seeing Debbie while Mum was alive depressed me more than anything else I had discovered about my father in the past few months. He couldn't put this indiscretion down to the inexperience of youth.

'Jesus, Dad. And I thought I knew you. First you have an affair with a seventeen-year-old, then you want her to have an abortion. Then when she refuses, you pay her off. Then you have an affair with your neighbour. You might as well go for the full house and tell me about my sister while you're in the mood to be so fucking honest.'

'Your sister?'

'My twin sister. Sue's other baby.'

Dad propped his pillow against the metal head-board of his hospital bed and sat up. 'What are you on about, our kid?'

'Don't give me that shit,' I said. 'Sue had twins. You did some deal with her. She kept the girl and you kept me.'

'Did she tell you that?' Dad looked confused. Uncertain.

'No, Mum told Lou before she died.'

'You're losing me.' Something told me he wasn't lying, so I told Dad how Mum had been worried for Sue and checked into her whereabouts. I described how she discovered that Sue was living in New Zealand with her daughter, who happened to be the same age as me.

'Have you talked to Sue?'

'No. I only heard about this a couple of days ago, just before the fire.'

Dad concentrated on his breathing for a few seconds. When he spoke, I had to strain to hear his words. 'I've got a daughter?'

Feeling guilty for having raised the issue with Dad while he was still recovering from the fire and from the loss of his lover, I left Dad and went in search of Vee.

Dad's and Vee's wards were on the same wing, but I still went down a few blind alleys before finding her.

The ward housing her cluster of beds was pretty identical to the one Dad was in. Women were lying in bed, some hooked up to drips, others hooked up to iPods. More grapes were in evidence on the women's ward than on the men's. As I walked towards Vee's bed, a flustered-looking nurse was finishing taking her blood pressure. She made a note on the chart at the end of the bed, nodded an acknowledgement to me and left.

'She was chatty,' I said after giving Vee's hand a squeeze.

'Shouldn't you be at work?' she asked through her wheezing.

'The boss's given me the day off. He's quite a nice guy when you get to know him, isn't he?'

Now it was Vee's turn to smile. She was looking a lot better than she had the previous day. Her eyes were less red and sunken. She had somehow managed to get hold of her make-up bag and hairbrush. There was now little visible evidence of her recent trauma other than a reddening around her Adam's apple.

The audible evidence was still there, though. Vee was in a similar condition to Dad, although her cough was worse. The tube that had kept her airway open had been removed the previous day, but her breathing was raspy and her voice croaky in the extreme.

I only spent an hour with Vee that afternoon, but that hour was important to me. With Vee not able to speak much, I had the freedom to get something that had kept me awake the previous night off my chest.

'Vee, your lover doesn't half snore. I don't know how you can sleep in the same house as him, let alone the same bed.'

With only a twitch of the mouth and a squeeze of the hand forthcoming from Vee, I moved on to the real reason for my detour to Vee's ward that day. 'I don't know how to say this, Vee, but you're the best.

210

Not many people would have done what you did in the face of that fire. It must have taken real courage. I don't know how I can ever thank you for what you've done.'

In danger of getting choked up myself, I ended my speech prematurely and hugged her lightly. She squeezed my shoulders before sitting back. '"You're the One That I Want",' she whispered.

My shock soon turned to a smile as I realised what Vee meant. She would have to go some to be in full voice by then, but if she wanted to sing 'You're the One That I Want' with me at Bren and Chelsea's wedding, then who was I to turn her down?

'You've got a deal,' I told her through gritted teeth.

Chapter Twenty-seven

Dad was discharged from hospital a couple of days later. On account of his lack of mobility, the doctors would only discharge him if he had someone to look after him. Dad pointed in my direction and I was too slow to hide behind a screen.

Within a couple of hours of running around after Dad, I scratched being a nursemaid for a living off the list of things I want to do when I grow up. Dad couldn't do anything for himself. The burns on his foot prevented him from walking. His fingers were too raw to grip crutches. All he could do was sit on the sofa, giving out orders. 'Pass the bottle.' 'Pass the crisps.' 'Pass my glasses.' He seemed to relish his newfound invalidity.

When Graham phoned suggesting a pint, I breathed a huge sigh of relief and passed the buck. Jezz was the lucky recipient.

'Why me?' he asked.

'Call it rent.'

I hadn't seen Graham since before Christmas. He was on good form and no longer held a grudge against me for sleeping with his ex-wife. 'No long-term damage done, except to your street cred,' he chortled when I brought the subject up. It was good to get out of the house, even if it did mean being subjected to Graham's brand of humour again.

There was no shortage of subjects for the pair of us to cover. We talked about the fire. Graham had only known Debbie to say hello to, but he managed to remain serious long enough to show the appropriate amount of sympathy.

When he learnt that Jezz was staying at my house until Vee was released from hospital, his sympathies seemed altogether more heartfelt. 'Living with that prick can't be easy.'

The story of Dad buying me for two thousand quid and the possibility of me having a sister were the next topics on the list. 'So this Sue didn't do a buy-one-get-one-free deal then,' he asked.

We had a more serious conversation about my ongoing mission to get back with Lou. 'She spent Christmas Day at mine,' I told him.

'If she chooses to spend Christmas with you, then you're practically a couple again. Presumably you shagged her?'

More serious, but not totally serious. When I told him it hadn't been that sort of a day, he didn't look particularly impressed.

'What's your strategy, Dave?' he asked. He was warming to the topic, sitting forward and practically rubbing his hands together with glee.

'What do you mean, "What's your strategy?"' There was no way I was going to tell him about Project Lou.

'Well, obviously you want Lou back. But let's see what you've done about it so far. You've got Helen pregnant. That certainly didn't help your cause. Then you've hung around Louise with your tongue hanging out. That isn't as bad as the Helen thing but it isn't working particularly well either, is it?'

'It's called being friendly, Graham.'

'My dog tries that approach all the time. It never works for him.'

God, how things change. Graham Hope was lecturing me on how to attract a woman. My indiscretion with his ex, as well as his relationship with the rich and ever so slightly stunning Amy, had sent his confidence levels through the roof. I sat back and blew out my cheeks. He hadn't finished.

'Lou's got you where she wants you. She can see you're desperate. That's unattractive, Dave. I should know, I spent the whole of last year being desperate.'

In for a penny, in for a pound. 'Go on then, Graham, tell me what you think I should do.'

'Treat 'em mean, keep 'em keen.' Generally, Graham was the least smug person I knew, but at that moment, he was looking smugger than a kid who'd corrected his teacher's spelling. He was literally rubbing his hands together with glee.

Not being able to bear any more lecturing from Graham, I was about to talk about something totally inane like world peace and happiness when I spotted a familiar face at the bar. My eyes had first been attracted to the gorgeous backside in the tight jeans. Only then had I clocked the face.

'It's my round,' I told Graham as I practically leapt to my feet.

Chelsea smiled as she saw me, but the uncertain look in her eyes told me she was struggling to place me. 'Dave, singing at your wedding,' I said, to help the process along.

'Oh yes, scatty weather girl,' she said in return, her eyes suddenly sparkling again.

As we were waiting to order, I quizzed Chelsea on how the final preparations for the wedding were going. 'Oh, it's all go at the moment. I had my bikini line done this morning and my practice hair appointment this afternoon.'

I wanted to ask about the former but, for once in my life, discretion trumped rashness. 'Practice hair appointment?'

'Yes, just to see what my hair will look like on the big day.' Her hair was long, shiny, straight and eminently hands-run-throughable, just as it had been the last time I saw it.

'It looks lovely,' I said.

Chelsea ordered a bottle of red and two glasses, then turned back to me. 'Everything's sorted. We're off to Reykjavik tomorrow on my hen weekend. What about the band? How's the set list coming along?'

'We've been rehearsing a lot in the last few weeks.' Putting a positive spin on things seemed preferable to panicking her with the news that one half of the band was laid up with smoke poisoning.

'Tell me some of the songs you're going to be playing.'

'We haven't finalised the set list yet. We are struggling on a few of the soppy ones.'

'Bren's the really soppy one. Maybe I can help you ditch a few of the slowies. Which ones are you struggling with?'

'"I Will Always Love You".' I put on my most sensual accent and stared into Chelsea's eyes as I said it.

'That's so unoriginal,' she laughed.

'"Kiss Me".'

'For fuck's sake, Dave, don't you ever give it a rest?' Lou said from over my right shoulder.

'Loose,' Chelsea called as my ex turned on her heel and retreated towards the exit.

By the time I had processed the fact that Lou was in the pub and that she and Chelsea knew each other, the two of them were out of the pub again. 'It's a fucking Ed Sheeran song,' I muttered as the door shut behind them.

Graham was staring at his phone, oblivious to the exchange that had just taken place at the bar. 'What the hell's this, you ponce,' he said as I put the bottle of red and two glasses on the table between us.

'Waste not, want not,' I said.

Jezz packed up his things and moved out of my house the following day. Looking after Dad was that bad. The part of me that liked having someone to share the workload with was sorry he had gone. The part of me that liked a good night's sleep wished he had pissed off the moment I returned from the pub. Even with a couple of pints and half a bottle of red inside me, I still couldn't block out Jezz's snoring. It was infinitely worse than Dad's coughing.

Vee left hospital the following day. She was on the mend but Jezz was pessimistic about her chances of regaining full use of her voice in time for Bren and Chelsea's wedding.

With none of us having any plans, we arranged a band get-together for New Year's Eve. Those of us who could sing and play would practise, those of us who couldn't would drink or just chill.

Our band get-together wasn't the only event organised for New Year's Eve. Debbie's funeral also took place that day. Ironically, it was at the same church as Mum's.

I was Dad's designated driver for the morning, his designated pusher too. At Dad's instruction, I parked his wheelchair in front of the first pew. Dad sat as near to the coffin as it was possible to get. There were a lot fewer mourners there than there had been for Mum's send-off. None of them asked Dad to move.

Jezz and I stood at the back and watched the service. Jezz shed a tear or two at his neighbour's funeral. I felt slightly detached. It wasn't that I resented Debbie for her part in their affair. I just didn't feel the love for her. I left that to Dad.

As the vicar gave a genuinely warm tribute to the deceased, I found myself gazing at Dad. Somehow I had managed to avoid snapping at him too often over the previous few days, but my reserves of willpower were dwindling fast.

Growing up, I had always worshipped my father. He was cool, up with modern culture and funny too, but it wasn't for those reasons that I worshipped him. What I idolised above anything else about him was his self-assuredness. He knew who he was. He didn't need, or even want, affirmation that what he was doing was right. He was totally comfortable in his own skin.

I have always wanted to be an individual, like Dad. I shunned university because I wanted to stick two fingers up to the school teachers who told me I was wasting my talents. Since entering the workplace, I have never kowtowed to my banking bosses. And in my domestic life, I have never thought too deeply, or even at all, about others' feelings. I didn't even see the signs before Lou walked out on me for God's sake.

Looking at Dad, sitting in the wheelchair at the front of the church, saying goodbye to his lover whose death he inadvertently caused, I realised why I hadn't got very far in life. Dad and I are different. Dad is self-assured because he's inherently selfish. He really doesn't care what others think of him, so long as he's happy. He is even willing to be dishonest in the pursuit of his happiness. I am built differently and should have realised it long before now. If I had, maybe I would have held on to Lou. I might even have had a more senior job.

As the funeral drew to a close and I moved to the front of the church to push Dad out into my waiting car, I realised my relationship with Dad would never return completely to the way it had been when Mum was still with us. Dad isn't the person I once thought he was. No doubt we will establish a new normal, a day-to-day way of coexisting that doesn't involve constant bickering and recrimination, but it won't be as warm and unquestioning as our relationship once was.

The wake was held at the Morden Brook. Luckily for me, Dad didn't want to go and share his memories of the deceased with a bunch of relative strangers. They probably got off lightly unless they were particularly interested in what their Auntie Debbie was like in bed.

During the afternoon, Jezz went back home to be with Vee. Despite being on Dad duty, I managed to knock up a pretty decent French onion soup for my guests. Dad had struggled with his food after the accident and I was guessing Vee would do likewise.

Dad had been drinking steadily since the funeral. By the time my fellow band members began arriving, he was fast asleep in my armchair. Feeling relieved, I shut the lounge door, hoping he would remain in the land of nod for the duration.

Vee and Jezz turned up on the dot of seven o'clock, followed a few minutes later by Jay. Jezz came armed with a bottle of champagne, and the proper stuff too, not your average chavvy Prosecco. Jay, on the other hand, brought a box of chocolate snowmen and a cheap bottle of plonk, both of which were probably unwanted Christmas presents.

As I was opening the fridge with the intention of putting the champagne somewhere cool until midnight, Jezz placed a hand on my arm. 'Bugger that, crack it open. It isn't every day I get engaged.'

The genuine congratulations and ritualistic backslapping that followed Jezz's announcement were much needed after the sombre mood of that morning's funeral. It was good to end the year on a high.

Jezz took great delight in telling us how he had got down on one knee that afternoon while Vee was in the bath.

'You dirty git, what did you propose to her when she was in the bath for?' Jay asked.

'I just fancied her, and it seemed right, that's all.'

'If she had said no, at least he could have drowned her,' Dad chirped up from the lounge. 'Someone bring me some scran.'

With the champagne and the respite of Dad's sleep over, I served the soup. Over dinner, we discussed our set list for Chelsea and Bren's wedding. Feeling emboldened by my conversation with the lovely Chelsea, I sought and enthusiastically received my fellow band members' agreement to ditch some of the more cringeworthy tracks from our plans.

'Bren won't be pleased,' Jay moaned as we struck off anything remotely wet.

'I'm more interested in pleasing Chelsea,' I responded.

'I bet you are,' was Jay's predictable response. On a related subject, Lou had texted me that morning, apologising for the misunderstanding in the pub. She also told me they were having a great time in Reykjavik.

Eventually, once we had finished off the soup and made a significant dent in our supply of cheap plonk, we adjourned to the garage to get down to some serious band business.

The three original band members experimented with a few new songs while Vee and Dad sat in dusty picnic chairs that hadn't seen a picnic in years. Ironically, 'You're the One That I Want' was the only song we were all agreed on, and even that depended upon Vee being up to it.

As we tried new songs, the two spectators would throw in the odd observation. To Vee, things were 'cool' or even 'awesome'. Dad's comments invariably included words like 'crap' and 'shite'.

Luckily for us, Dad passed out drunk again well before midnight, so we ended the night feeling good, awesome even, about ourselves.

Chapter Twenty-eight

Most of my New Year's morning was spent running around after Dad. 'Can I have some coffee?' 'Have you got any headache tablets?' 'What's for breakfast?'

When I wasn't being Dad's gofer, I was replying to the million inane and only vaguely coherent text messages I received as Big Ben was signalling the start of another year. Some wise sage once said that you can judge a man by the company he keeps. If my friends are busy texting each other at midnight on New Year's Eve then I am a sad git. Couldn't they put their phones down and have fun for once in their lives?

One of the texts I received was from Sue. 'Happy NY. How about seeing the next one in together?'

It was lunchtime when I read Sue's message. According to my mental arithmetic, that meant it would be just before midnight in New Zealand. With the pub to sort, Sue shouldn't yet have turned in for the night. Texting wouldn't get me the answers I needed from her, so I decided to give her a ring.

Not wanting Dad to overhear our conversation, I retreated to my car to make the call.

My calculations proved right. Sue answered pretty quickly. We exchanged greetings and discussed our various celebrations before I moved the conversation on to altogether more tricky subjects. 'Have I got a twin sister?'

There was silence on the other end of the phone. 'Sue?'

'Yes.' I might have been reading too much into that one word, but Sue's tone sounded resigned.

'Why didn't you tell me about her when I came to see you?'

'It's complicated, David. I...'

'It's not complicated. It's pretty bloody simple.' I was fed up now. 'My dad's a scheming git and you're just as bad. My mother was so much better than the pair of you. As far as I'm concerned, you and Dad can go to hell.' Not only did I disconnect the call, but I banged the car horn with my forehead for good measure.

When I went back inside, Dad was watching the telly. A huge woman was being goaded by a personal trainer-type to walk faster down the street. 'Dangle a bar of chocolate in front of her and she'd soon speed up,' Dad said as he noticed me.

The remote was on the coffee table beside him. Wanting his full attention, I muted the sound. 'I just talked to your former lover.'

His eyebrows rose momentarily until he cottoned on that I was talking about Sue, not Debbie or whoever else he had formerly loved. 'And?'

'And I hung up on her.'

'Why?'

'Because I'm sick of being told a bunch of half-truths and bullshit, that's why. Lou told me Mum hadn't asked you about Sue having twins because she was fed up of hearing your lies. That's where I'm at. I can't be arsed with it anymore.'

'But what about your sister?'

'I've gone my entire life without knowing she existed. So what, I've got a sister. I'll get over it. I've got my own life to lead.'

'I've got a daughter too. I want to know about her. I've got a right to know about her.'

'You've got a right. You're having a laugh, Dad. How come you've got a right to know about your daughter but I didn't have a right to know about my mother? And Sue didn't have any right to know about me as I grew up, did she?' I knew I was winding myself up, but sometimes you have no choice but to give in to your emotions.

'Son, you don't understand.'

'The one thing I admire Sue for is getting one over on you all those years ago. She got you to pay her a shedload of money. You thought you were buying her baby but she only sold you half the goods. I bet she was laughing when she left me with you. She'd got her money, and she still had a baby to bring up. She had her precious daughter.'

Dad studied me for a bit before looking back towards the screen. The obese woman was now on a treadmill, her fat wobbling as she jogged. That machine must have had some motor.

As he reached for the remote to unmute the sound, Dad asked if he could talk to Sue. 'Do what you like,' I told him, 'it's a free country.'

After looking after Dad, returning to work after Christmas was a blessed relief. With quite a few of my colleagues hearing about it for the first time after their holidays, the fire was the talk of the banking hall. By lunchtime, despite the seriousness of the event itself, some of the stories I was overhearing were making me chuckle.

The conversation that really caught my attention was the one between Ditsy Melanie and Pritti, stand-in for the week while Vee recovered from the effects of the smoke. 'Oh Jeremy's such a hero. He ran into the burning house, fought off the fire and rescued a man from almost certain death.'

'How brave.'

'But he didn't stop there. He went back in and carried Vee out over his shoulder, like a proper fireman.'

'How romantic.'

'And then he asks her to marry him. He's so hot.'

'They get on like a house on fire, don't they?'

The flames didn't particularly need fanning, but sometimes opportunities are too good to miss. 'His dressing gown caught fire when he was rescuing Vee,' I told them. 'When he carried her out into the street, he was totally naked.'

'Totally naked. Wow, that's so romantic.'

'They should give him a medal.'

'But what would they hang it on?' I asked as I left them to masturbate, sorry adulate, in peace.

On the way home from work, Lou messaged me asking if I fancied dinner somewhere in Wimbledon. With only Dad's incessant requests to go home to, I was happy to say yes. Let's face it, even if there had been hordes of Swedish au pairs waiting for me at home, I would still have been more than happy to have dinner with Lou.

It was only a short walk up the hill to Wagamama. As I walked into the restaurant, I couldn't help thinking that it was a strange choice of venue for the evening on Lou's part. The buzz of chatter emanating from the long communal tables would make intimate conversation difficult.

Looking around, I couldn't see Lou. The restaurant was busy and my choice of table limited. I selected two seats next to a bunch of young professional types grabbing a meal after a hard day's work. It was either that or perching at the end of a pew full of raucous children celebrating little Johnny's birthday.

The stakes were high that night. Some of the obstacles to Lou and me being together seemed to be disappearing. Lou knew the score about me. She knew I still wanted her. She knew my feelings on the Helen thing. If she was to be believed, and I had no reason to doubt her, she had split up with the book dork. So, in my mind at least, if things didn't work out, then it was because she wasn't interested.

By the time Lou eventually graced me with her presence, the shirts and ties next to me had been replaced by a gang of babbling beauties having a pre-theatre meal, and I had started on my third bottle of lager. It was hot in the restaurant. I always drink faster when I'm nervous too, and I was certainly nervous that night. Not because of the gang of babbling beauties but because of the high stakes.

As so often happens, Lou's entrance disturbed the equilibrium in the busy restaurant. Men stopped mid-conversation and stared. Women stared too, but their faces displayed different emotions. I am no expert on fashion but by my reckoning, Lou could have walked straight out of a Vogue photoshoot. She oozed high fashion. She demanded attention. She sat opposite me.

'Sorry I'm late, my last meeting dragged on.' Doing my best to hide my irritation at being kept waiting for so long in the hot and noisy restaurant, I kissed Lou, politely rather than passionately. Lou then clocked the babbling beauties. 'I wonder why you chose this table.'

For some reason, it was probably the lager, Graham's smug voice popped into my head as Lou smiled at me. Was there really anything in what he was saying?

Doing my best to push such thoughts out of my mind and calm myself down, I asked Lou how she knew Chelsea.

'She's Geoff's sister.'

'The book dork?'

'Geoffrey.'

'Ah. Wait a minute,' I said, catching up quickly, 'does that mean the book dork will be coming to Chelsea's wedding?'

'I expect so.'

'Fantastic.' The thought of performing in front of the book dork stressed me out even more.

'I didn't know you were playing at the reception until Chelsea explained the "I Will Always Love You" and "Kiss" references,' Lou explained. 'Can't you get out of it?'

'No.' Of course I couldn't get out of it, not without letting a lot of people down at least. And in any case, as I sat there opposite Lou, part of me began to relish the chance of being centre stage for an evening in front of my wife while he was only a bit-part player.

To diffuse things, I changed tack slightly. 'How can someone called Geoffrey have a sister called Chelsea?'

Lou just shrugged before changing the subject herself. 'Reykjavik was great fun, thanks for asking.'

'So was my New Year's Eve with Dad, thanks for asking.' I could hear Graham's voice again, chuntering away at the margins of my consciousness. Don't be the dog with his tongue hanging out.

'We went on a pub crawl.'

'That's a shocker for a hen party.' My third bottle of lager was empty by now.

'Then we went and soaked in the blue lagoon. We were practically in the Arctic Circle, it was the middle of winter and we were in our bikinis.'

'I bet Chelsea looked hot.'

Lou had been following her own agenda, oblivious to what I had been saying. But she was gradually beginning to notice I wasn't being my normal easy-going self. In the heat of the restaurant, sweat, rather than desperation, was oozing from my every pore.

'Do you fancy Chelsea?'

'What, for the Premier League, unfortunately yes.'

'Why are you being a twat, Dave?'

'Am I being a twat? Sorry.' I was sorry, but I couldn't seem to stop myself. 'I love her nickname for you, by the way.'

'What?'

'Chelsea called you "Loose" the other night in the pub.' I raised my arm to attract the waitress's attention. 'Shall we order?'

'Do you know what, I don't think I'll bother,' Lou said. As they had done only minutes before, people stopped to watch Lou as she departed. Despite our conversation, she was as graceful when she left as she had been when she arrived. I ended up eating my green chicken curry out of a carton on the 163 bus on my way home. What an arse. I don't know what came over me. Why on earth had I followed Graham Hope's dating advice? That's like listening to a virgin telling you how to have great sex. Just as the obstacles to us getting back together were dispersing, I had yet again done my best to construct another one.

'That's the last time I take dating advice from you,' I texted Graham later that evening.

'Stick with it. It won't work overnight,' came the response. I don't think so.

Chapter Twenty-nine

A succession of band rehearsals over the following week prevented me from dwelling too much on how I had messed things up with Lou. Our playing order for the wedding of the century was coming together. Much to my fellow band members' consternation, 'Bohemian Rhapsody' and 'In the Air Tonight' hadn't made the final cut. 'They're hardly going to get people up dancing, are they?' I argued.

Vee's voice was gradually returning to its pre-fire huskiness. She was still prone to the occasional coughing fit when she spoke, so singing at the reception was a long shot. One good thing to come out of the fire was that Vee's throat irritation wasn't conducive to smoking.

Returning to work proved to be a big fillip for Vee. She was given a standing ovation as she made her way into the banking hall, with Jezz at her side. 'Re-enact the fire, Jeremy. Strip off and carry her over your shoulder,' Ditsy Melanie shouted, making herself heard over the applause.

'What's she on about?' Vee asked Jezz.

'Don't ask.' Jezz was ever so slightly red.

My birthday came and went with little incident. Dad, who was gradually working out a way of getting about without putting too much weight on the sole of his left foot, surprised me by having dinner ready when I got home from work. Pork chops, mash and peas.

Dad and I had managed not to piss each other off too much in the days leading up to my birthday. Neither of us mentioned the sister/daughter thing. Part of me was relieved, but another part that I couldn't completely suppress wanted to talk about it. After I'd cleared up the birthday dinner detritus, I gave my inner voice an airing.

'Sue hasn't been in touch today. I would've thought she'd have at least sent me a text.'

'I wouldn't worry about it, son.'

'She's probably too busy celebrating with my sister.' Instead of responding, Dad put the telly on. So much for talking.

The other person who didn't contact me was Lou. To be fair, after my 'treat 'em mean' experiment, the onus was undoubtedly on me to make the next move.

Although most of what Graham had said that night in the pub was bollocks, the one thing I couldn't completely dismiss was his dog analogy. There was nothing less attractive than a desperate woman. Likewise, there must be nothing more off-putting than a desperate man.

I was a prat towards Lou in Wimbledon. That was stupid. But I was determined not to sniff Lou's arse with my tongue hanging out either. The upshot of all that philosophising was that I didn't text Lou.

Mum's absence was particularly noticeable on my birthday. She always used to make a fuss of me. Even when I was a grown man, old enough to vote, drive and have sex (I never did them all at the same time), Mum would still insist on baking me a cake. The one concession she did make over the years was replacing the Smartie-laden chocolate monstrosity with a carrot or perhaps coffee variety. She would often turn up unannounced and gatecrash whatever celebrations I was engaging in, with the cake being her admission fee. I never minded her gatecrashing though, because everyone loved Mum and thought she was cool.

Feeling guilty that I hadn't been to visit her on my birthday, I vaulted over the wrought-iron cemetery railings the following evening after work. It was pitch black and bloody freezing; Chelsea was predicting snow. My gloves stuck to the ice-cold metal as I manoeuvred myself over the unwelcoming spikes.

Mum's plot was looking well maintained. I was surprised to see a single red rose resting against the recently installed headstone. Was Dad that mobile? The gold lettering stood out clearly in London's ambient night-time glow. 'Valerie Fazackerley, beloved wife, mother and friend.'

My own bunch of flowers, bought from outside Raynes Park station, was already beginning to look a bit sad as I placed it next to Dad's rose on Mum's grave.

Four months had passed since Mum died. Losing someone is an odd thing. My grief wasn't quite as all-encompassing as it had been in the days and weeks after Mum's death. Maybe I was learning to cope with it. Things don't necessarily get easier every day though. Some days are good, others less so. One day I would be peeved that an eighty-year-old celebrity convicted of abusing children is still alive whereas Mum died in her early seventies. The next day, if I heard of someone dying young, I would thank my lucky stars that Mum enjoyed life for as long as she did.

A real fear of frostbite prevented me from staying with Mum for too long. As I walked through the cemetery, back towards the streetlights and the sound of cars accelerating away from the Beverley roundabout, back towards the land of the living, I heard a dog barking. It was the Hope boys' German Shepherd, Albus. Jack and Sean were in their front garden, teasing the dog with a football.

Helen and I hadn't seen each other since that Saturday before Christmas in Topsham. Despite all that was going on in my life, putting the abortion out of my mind was proving difficult. On impulse, I walked up Helen's drive and banged on her front door.

'Have you brought the condoms with you this time?' Sean asked as he jogged past me to fetch the ball.

'Touché.'

Helen was surprised to see me. Judging by her frown, she wasn't particularly delighted either. 'I've come to apologise,' I told her.

'What for?' She opened her door wider and invited me in.

'I don't know really, the whole thing I suppose. Giving out the wrong signals, being irresponsible, not being supportive.'

'I'll put the kettle on, shall I?' As Helen made the coffees, I looked around her homely front room. The room was dominated by a long oak table and high-backed chairs. Photos of the boys were arranged neatly on the matching oak sideboard. One picture in particular caught my eye. It was of Helen and Graham signing the registry book at their wedding. I wished I had kept Lou's and my wedding photos instead of smashing them up in a fit of pique when she ran off with the dork. The aggressive act felt good at the time, but I have regretted it many times since.

'Why have you really come?' Helen asked as she placed two huge mugs of milky coffee on the table.

'Just to make sure you're OK.' My hands were freezing despite the gloves. I wrapped them around my mug.

'You want releasing from your guilt, don't you?'

'I do feel guilty. Don't you?'

'I'm fine, Dave. We aren't the first people to make a baby and decide it's not right to go through with it. We've just got to deal with it.'

I nodded. My guilt was proving hard to shake off, maybe because Helen and I had done what Dad had wanted to do when Sue was pregnant with me. A little boy or girl would never see the light of day because of us. He or she would never cry or smile, never take those faltering first steps, never go to school, never have a first snog behind the bike sheds.

My guilt wasn't the only thing on my mind that night, though. 'Can I ask you another question? Was it mine?'

'Fuck off, Dave.'

Helen's reaction didn't surprise me, but for some reason, I couldn't stop myself from asking.

Part Seven

Dave Fazackerley

Chapter Thirty

'What the hell?'

I got the shock of my life when I got back from my trip to Helen's via the cemetery. The telly wasn't on. That wasn't the shock but it was how I knew things weren't normal. Instead of being greeted by a torrent of inane chatter, music or gunfire, I was greeted by an almost oppressive silence.

Through the hall, I could see Dad sitting in what had become his usual spot, my solitary armchair. It was only when I walked into the lounge that I saw who else was there.

'Hello, David.'

'Sue. What are you doing here?'

'Sorry I missed your birthday. I hope you don't mind me coming, even if it's a day late. I spent most of yesterday flying.'

It took me a while to get my head around the situation. Sue shouldn't have been in my house, but there she was, perched on the edge of the sofa, an empty coffee mug on her lap and her travel bag at her feet.

Did I mind her coming? As it turns out, no, I didn't. No one has ever travelled across the world to see me before. It showed she cared. On that basis alone, I was pleased to see her. We hugged, slightly formally but not overly so.

Looking from Sue to Dad, the prevailing mood wasn't immediately obvious. Neither looked angry, neither looked happy.

'Well, this is nice,' I said, sitting down next to Sue. 'If my sister was here, we'd have a full house.'

'That's why I'm here,' Sue started.

Dad cut her off. 'She's dead.'

'Dead?'

No wonder neither of them looked happy. My head felt muddled. Losing a sister should be a big deal, but not knowing her made a difference. Sue's loss was palpable, though. Her face was reddening as she rummaged in her bag. She produced a leather case and opened it, revealing two faded baby photos, presumably one of me and the other of my sister.

All wrapped up, we looked pretty similar, pink-faced with random strands of dark hair high up on our foreheads. We were both lying in an otherwise empty suitcase, with one of us in the base and the other in the lid.

Sue pointed to the baby wrapped in red. 'That's you. I only had one blanket so I had to wrap you in my jumper.'

'What was she called?'

'Teresa. Teresa Elsmere.'

'Terri,' Dad chipped in. Even with my back turned to him, I knew he was smirking. 'But with an i.'

'How did she die, Sue?'

'Mainly it was leukaemia, but it was pneumonia that finished her off. She died last year.' Sue was sitting bolt upright. Blinking back the tears, she was determined to keep her composure. There was obviously something she wanted to get off her chest.

'Why didn't you tell me about her?'

'She died on the twenty-third of September,' Dad interrupted from over my left shoulder.

'That's when...'

'Val died, yes.'

I turned to look at Dad but he had sat back in his chair, quiet again. Until the next time he felt like taking over the story.

'I don't know why I didn't tell you,' Sue answered. 'There were lots of reasons and there were no reasons. There were times I wanted to tell you, but each time, something stopped me.

'A lot came down to shame. You never had the chance to meet your sister, and that was my fault. I chose to take Terri back to New Zealand, not you. I was ashamed of that. And God knows why, but I was ashamed I didn't tell your dad about his daughter too.'

'Too bloody right you should be.' Dad's interruptions were getting on my nerves, but I took my lead from Sue and just ignored him.

'When it came down to it, when you were sitting in front of me, I just couldn't bring myself to tell you.'

'Did she, Teresa, know about me?'

'When she got ill, yes, I told her. She desperately wanted to meet you.' Sue was still doing her best to hold herself together. The occasional tear escaped, only to be quickly wiped away.

'I could have flown over to meet her.'

'You didn't know about me at the time, let alone her. Anyway, I knew Valerie was ill. We couldn't intrude.'

'How did you know Mum was ill?'

'Because she's on my bloody Facebook.' Dad again.

'What?' The conversation was beginning to move too fast. Facebook is a mystery to me. Preferring to talk to people face to face rather than via a computer or a phone, I haven't bothered with it. Sue explained that she had created a dummy account a few years ago with the intention of befriending me and keeping up with my life. She hadn't found me so she befriended Dad instead. For some reason, Dad friended her back, or whatever it is you do.

'So you knew when I got married,' I asked, getting side-tracked from the main event.

'No, but I knew when you split up. And I knew when Valerie was ill.'

'You told your daughter about me but she couldn't contact me. What was the point in telling her?'

'There was a point.' Something at the bottom of her coffee mug was attracting her attention. It was the first time in the conversation that Sue hadn't been making eye contact.

'Because you wanted to cleanse yourself before she died? Because it was the right thing to do?'

'Because there was a chance she might not die.'

'I don't understand.'

'Can I ask you a question, David?'

'You just did.' Dad was determined to let us know he was still there.

'Shut the fuck up, Dad.' My stare was, if anything, more venomous than my words.

'David,' Sue took my hand, 'were you a bone marrow donor?'

'Yes, how did...' And then it hit me.

240

Sue nodded. That appeared to have been the answer she was expecting. Upon hearing it, her self-control dissolved, her dam of composure burst by a wave of emotion, a torrent of silent tears. She hugged herself tightly as she cried.

There was little I could do other than to supply her with tissues once her shudders had passed. Dad hoisted himself up and went into the kitchen. I wasn't sorry to see him go.

Once Sue had regained her composure, she picked up from where we had left off. She explained that Terri was really poorly. The doctors diagnosed her with acute myeloid leukaemia. Her body wasn't producing enough healthy white blood cells. Finding a compatible bone marrow donor was her best hope of survival.

'One of the first questions Terri was asked when they started talking about receiving someone else's stem cells was, "Have you got any siblings?" Naturally, she said no. Later, I told the doctor about you. He said they check out the UK and other bone marrow registers as a matter of course anyway.'

I nodded. 'I was on the UK register.'

'They found an excellent match from the UK,' Sue confirmed, 'but they wouldn't tell us any more details. Excellent matches are as rare as rocking horse shit, so I knew in my heart it was you.'

Dad hobbled in with a fresh mug of coffee for Sue. She took a sip. It was getting late but I was transfixed by her story. She went on to describe how Terri had been in hospital for a week, receiving both chemotherapy and radiotherapy to prepare her body for the transplant.

'One night, Terri looked so frail and weak in her hospital bed that I worried she wouldn't survive long enough to receive the healthy bone marrow. My will broke and I told her about you.'

'And me?' Dad asked.

'Why would I want to tell her about you?'

Dad went back to his sulk while Sue carried on with her story.

'Terri was quick. Straight away she asked whether it was your stem cells she was going to receive.

'Knowing about you gave her the strength to carry on. She received the new bone marrow and was doing really well for a while. But then she got an infection. The infection developed into pneumonia. Her immune system had been dampened down so her body would accept the new bone marrow, but that meant she couldn't fight the infection. She got gradually worse until eventually she couldn't fight it any longer.'

Mum was always into helping people. Our whole family were regular blood donors. When I was younger, Mum persuaded me to donate my sperm too. Donating sperm was, for me, just a routine. I never gave a thought to the idea that there might be baby Daves in existence. Donating bone marrow took a bit more effort, but, until that night, I had thought about it in a similar manner. Although I felt a better person for having done it, I hadn't wondered too much about the recipient of my healthy tissue. As a result, Sue's story was hard to take in.

We talked a bit more that evening, about how Sue hadn't known for certain she was having twins until the actual event. She told us, and Dad in particular, how she had struggled to look after herself, let alone her twins, in those traumatic first few weeks. She also explained how her friend Rebecca had looked after Terri whenever Sue was meeting dad to discuss money.

Once Sue became two thousand pounds richer but one baby poorer, she had travelled back to New Zealand and to her mum as quickly as she could.

Sue told us about Terri, too. Like her mother, all Terri had wanted to do for a living was sing. She pursued her dream, spending much of her life as a backing singer, following the work across Australia. When she wasn't singing on commercials or as a backing vocalist, she would undertake whatever voiceover work she could get. She served her time on the Australian pub singing circuit too, especially when she was younger.

'Was she married?' Dad asked.

'Yes, but he was a prick. It didn't last long,' Sue replied.

All in all, my sister sounded like an unremarkable but decent person who led an interesting life. She was someone I would have liked to meet.

By the end of the evening, I for one was numb. Sue was scheduled to stay in a hotel down the road, next to the municipal swimming baths, but, not being particularly keen to expose herself to the freezing air of a British winter's night, she willingly accepted my offer of the second spare room for the night instead.

As Dad hobbled off to his room, Sue helped me carry the empty mugs into the kitchen. She watched me load the dishwasher. As Dad's door shut upstairs, Sue went to her purse.

'Terri wrote you a letter before she passed.'

Chapter Thirty-one

The next few days were mostly taken up with last-minute band rehearsals, work and refereeing fights between Sue and Dad. Even though it meant she was in the same house as Dad, Sue ended up staying with me rather than checking into the sad and depressing motel down the road.

As each day passed, Sue would ask me whether I had read Terri's letter. Feeling punch-drunk, it took me a couple of days to motivate myself. The last such letter from a dead relative had changed the course of my life. I was slightly reluctant to open a fresh can of worms but, in the end, despite not having known her, what Terri had to say did interest me. A couple of days before the wedding of the year, after the oldies had gone to bed, I sat at my dining table and tore open the envelope.

Dear David,
My brother, this is a hard letter to write. Not just because I am physically frail and tired, but because I have so much I want to say to you. I will try and stay focussed, but forgive me if my mind wanders.

If you are reading this, you must already know something about your other family. Did Mum tell you? I urged her to. She has had a decent life, but I know now why she sometimes has a faraway look in her eyes. I know where she goes in her dreams. You have always been in her thoughts. She shouldn't bottle things up anymore.

Mike, Mum's husband, was an awesome man. Mum and Mike married when I was very young. He was kind, fun, clever and generous. Even though Mum told me he wasn't my father, I called him Dad. He was always there for me.

Occasionally, I would ask Mum about my real dad, but he was only ever a curiosity to me. Mum was quite open about some things. She told me how the two of them met. She told me he was a hotshot musician in London. She didn't tell me his name though.

Mike's death knocked Mum for six. She hit the bottle pretty hard. I lived with her for a few months and did my best to keep the Silver Fern running smoothly. One day, Mum was too far gone to do her own banking so she gave me the combination to her safe. When I opened it, I came across photographs of two babies, each lying in the same open suitcase, one in the base, the other in the lid. Instantly, I knew I had a twin.

There was a third photo too, of Mum gazing into a handsome man's eyes in front of a lake full of rowing boats. The image told me a lot about our mum and dad's love for each other, as did the inscriptions they had each scribbled on the back.

'Terry Fazackerley, I love you till the twelfth of never.'

'Mouldy old dough x.'

Discovering my father's name gave me a lead to follow to find out more. For a while, I did nothing with this new information. Although I desperately wanted to know about my twin, my time was fully occupied looking after Mum and running the pub. Even when Mum pulled herself together and gave up drinking, I still couldn't bring myself to ask her about you. I didn't want to give her reason to slip back into her alcoholic haze.

Instead, when I knew Mum was strong enough to cope without me, I used some money Mike left me in his will to book a flight to London. It wasn't difficult to find my dad. It wasn't hard to find you either.

Your dad rarely seemed to stray far from home during my fortnight in London. When he did go out, it was with his wife, who looked frail and in pain. I didn't have a clue whether our dad even knew I existed, so I couldn't just go up to him and introduce myself.

You were different though. In the same way I hadn't known I had a brother, I was pretty sure you didn't know you had a sister. You seemed to go out a lot. I watched you for a couple of evenings in the pub by the railway station near your house. My heart was telling me to talk to you but my head said back off. My head was just about winning until you spotted me and asked if I wanted a drink.

Do you remember me? In my panic, I intro-duced myself as Elisa. Elisa is actually my best friend from Melbourne. You thought I was from Australia. I didn't correct you.

We had a few drinks together. You told me

about your life, about your band and your job. As the evening drew on, you also told me about your ex. And then you told me about your mum being diagnosed with cancer. It was at that point I knew I couldn't come clean with you. You had enough on your plate without me adding a sister and a totally new mother into the mix.

It was great to meet up with you a few times while I was in London. I loved getting to know you. You are so much like me. You like a laugh, you like to have fun and you love your singing. I have been lucky enough to make a decent living out of my voice over the years.

I was sad to leave London, but I had to go. My life was in New Zealand and Australia. And I couldn't stay around you for too long without having to explain why I didn't want to kiss you.

I began feeling tired and frail pretty soon after I got back to New Zealand. Things progressed quickly from there, and pretty soon I needed a bone marrow transplant and the doctors were asking me whether I had any siblings. There was no way I wanted to disturb you while your adopted mother was battling her own illness, so I pretended not to know about you.

Mum eventually came clean with me a few weeks ago, when I was at a particularly low ebb. She had already come clean with the doctors too. She didn't have a clue I knew about my brother already. When I was drinking with you in London, Mum thought I was in Australia visiting Elisa. It would be overstating things to say I felt guilty about seeing you when I knew Mum hadn't, but I didn't feel confident *enough about my actions to share them with her either. She would have been upset.*

There is a high chance I have received your stem cells. It doesn't surprise me you were on a list of potential donors. From the little I know about you, you seem like a kind and generous person for whom helping others comes naturally.

I'm gutted I didn't get to know about you when we were younger. We could have had so much fun. We could have sung together, I could have beaten you at sports and embarrassed you in front of your mates. Isn't that what sisters do?

Mum tells me I'm fifteen minutes older than you. It's every older sister's right to bully, nag and generally annoy their younger brother. I have been denied that opportunity. If I were to nag you now, I would tell you to shave your head more frequently than you do. Your balding pate isn't a good look unless it's clean shaven.

I would nag you about your chat-up lines too. Us women like to feel special in our own right. When you constantly bang on about your ex all the time, it tends to turn us off. If you really do want to get back with your ex then stop pissing about and do something about it.

There, I have fulfilled my sisterly duty. I wish I could have done it more, it's quite good fun.

I may yet pull through this bout of illness, but from the way the doctors frown when they look at my chart, I don't think the odds are in my favour. If I do pull through, and I am determined to do so, I will rip this letter up and travel to England to talk to you again in person.

But if I don't, then I want you to promise me something. Don't waste your life. Pursue your dreams. Go after what you want. Don't settle for second best. Life's too short.
Your sister,
Terri

Elisa.

Elisa and I only spent a few evenings together, but in that short period of time, she had managed to get under my skin.

My interest in Elisa, or Terri as I now know her to be, was definitely more mental than physical. She was interesting to talk to. We shared a common love for music in particular. We shared a similar sense of humour too. She was also genuinely interested in me. That in itself was a refreshing change from most of my other post-Lou dates.

Even though the attraction was more mental than physical, as it has turned out, I did still try and kiss my own sister. Cringing, I recalled the awkwardness of my repelled advance outside the Raynes Park Tavern. As I leant in to kiss her, Terri put her hand on my cheek. 'It's not going to happen,' she told me in no uncertain terms.

At least after reading her letter, I could put a face to my sister's name. And it was a face that was so obviously similar to Sue's that I couldn't believe I had missed the connection.

I met Elisa before I knew of Sue's existence. And when I met Sue, Elisa was so far from my thoughts that there was no chance of me spotting the similarities in hair colour, eyes, laughter lines and smiles.

Reading Terri's letter, and realising that I had met her, gave my sister meaning in my mind. I would never feel Sue's level of pain about her death, but, as I sat there at my dining table staring at Terri's letter, I felt a sense of loss that I hadn't previously felt. The two of us would have got on. We would have had a laugh together. We would have been there for each other, as twins often are.

Before turning the downstairs lights off and going up to bed, I promised my sister I would pursue my dreams.

Chapter Thirty-two

The e-list celebrity wedding of the year was upon us. The editorial team from Weather Forecasting Weekly needed to contain their excitement no longer.

I woke up early that Saturday. Normally it's hard to sleep on the day of a gig, but what woke me at the crack of dawn wasn't anything to do with the band. It wasn't anything to do with my sister either.

What prevented me from sleeping any later than the milkman was the realisation that Bren and Chelsea's wedding reception could be make or break time for Lou and me.

Project Lou wasn't progressing smoothly. If truth be told, since I made a noodle of myself in Wimbledon, it wasn't progressing at all. But that was about to change. I had a feeling that being in the presence of both Lou and the book dork at the same time would bring things to a head one way or another.

Lou and I had only spoken once since my treat 'em mean experiment. She phoned me a couple of nights before the wedding. Not wanting to miss an opportunity, and totally disregarding Graham's advice to the contrary, I jumped in quickly and apologised for my ignorant behaviour.

'What was the matter with you?' she asked.

'PMT.' Pre-Meal Tension, Post-Mum Trauma, my Prick of a Mate's a Twat.

Lou wasn't interested in having an extended inquest into my performance. She quickly moved the conversation on to more important matters. 'Don't punch Geoff at the wedding, will you.'

'Why not, the guy's an idiot.'

'It would spoil Chelsea's day. She is his sister after all.'

'OK, I promise I won't punch the dork.'

'Geoff.'

'Whatever his name is, I promise I won't punch him. Are you still sleeping in the spare room?'

'Are you still sleeping with your best mate's ex?'

Our last conversation was hardly conclusive proof that the two of us were meant to be together. But I didn't need proof. I just knew.

Jay, Jezz and Vee arrived at my house at one. By then, I had second-guessed Project Lou, sworn at Dad three times and was on my fourth coffee. I did my best to focus on the gig, and managed it for the next five minutes at least.

We were due to pitch up at the venue and set up while everyone else was at the registry office enjoying the nuptials. That gave us just over an hour to test one or two things out, including Vee's ability to sing.

Taking our lead from Premier League football teams, we had put off Vee's fitness test until the very last minute, giving her every possible chance to recover from her hamstring injury before the match, or in her case, her smoke inhalation before the gig.

Unfortunately for Vee, she didn't pass the test. She got raspy halfway through the first verse of 'You're the One That I Want', and eventually had to step away and concentrate on her breathing. Her mind was willing, but her lungs weren't able. Reluctantly, she accepted that her role for the evening would be limited to making sure Jezz didn't get too pissed too early, a difficult enough task in itself.

'We'll just have to go to plan B then, won't we?' Dad observed as Jezz was consoling Vee.

'God no,' I groaned, 'not this again.'

In anticipation that Vee would fail her fitness test, Dad had come up with plan B a few days before the wedding. It was a fairly simple plan really. 'Me and Sue could sing that shit,' he had suggested, referring to the Grease number.

'You are joking, aren't you?' Sue hadn't been impressed.

'Why not? You had a great voice way back when. You'd do a grand job.'

'It's not my voice I'm worried about. I object to singing "You're the One That I Want" to you. It's just not right.' Sue shook her head disbelievingly.

From Sue's reaction, the rest of us had assumed Dad's plan was dead in the water, but half an hour before we were due to pack up our gear and head for the gig, he and Sue showed us how mistaken our assumption had been.

At Dad's insistence, Jay, Jezz and I played the track, and Dad and Sue put on a show that rolled back the years. Sue had a better voice than Dad, but both had great presence. As I watched them, I could even pick up a hint of the chemistry that must have existed between them some forty years previously. Every so often though, Sue checked herself and frowned at

Dad, presumably just to keep him in his place.

At the end of their performance, Dad and Sue didn't exactly receive a standing ovation, but there were certainly a few surprised looks on our faces.

'What do you reckon,' Dad said, patting me on the back, 'has your old man still got it or what?'

'You've been practising?'

Sue smiled at me. 'You get that on the big jobs.'

'It's still not exactly hip though, is it,' Jay cautioned, 'the two of you are hardly John and Olivia, are you?'

'As if you lot have ever been hip,' Vee chipped in. She had a point.

Dad wasn't finished yet, either. 'It could be one for the grandparents. I bet the reception'll be full of old gits like us.'

'Speak for yourself.' Sue didn't like being aged by Dad.

In the end, we took a vote and Life in the Faz Lane unanimously decided to include Dad and Sue's rendition of 'You're the One That I Want' on our set list.

As we loaded our kit into Jay's van and headed off towards North Cheam, our confidence was high. After months of practising, we were ready.

Other than the Grease track, our set list included a mixture of our usual 80s repertoire and, at Boring Bren's request, some more modern stuff. Our interpretation of modern was a fairly loose one – anything from 1990 onwards. Our modern stuff included 5 Seconds of Summer's 'She Looks So Perfect', Ed Sheeran's 'Photograph' and The Kings of Leon's 'Sex on Fire', as well as songs by Elbow and The Calling. Bren and Chelsea's family and friends were in for a treat.

Although there was no sign of the Weather Forecasting Weekly's paparazzi at the social club as we turned up with all our gear, the venue was bustling with activity. Kids were playing football outside while their responsible adults were either standing on the walkway having a fag or making use of the subsidised bar. It took all of our combined efforts to stop our own irresponsible adults, namely Jezz and Dad, from joining the drinkers for 'a quick snifter'.

We hadn't been invited to the wedding breakfast (we were really gutted to be missing Boring Bren's speech), so once our gear was set up and we had done a few rudimentary sound checks, we nipped out for a bit of pre-gig dinner. Not wanting to constrict my diaphragm, while the wedding guests were enjoying chicken stroganoff followed by profiteroles, I tolerated poached egg on toast with Sue. The guitarist and the drummer opted for kebabs and chips.

'It's custom,' Jezz protested when Sue raised a half-hearted objection, 'and besides, if there's a free bar, I'll need something substantial to line my stomach.'

The function room was in the process of being transformed from a sit-down eating venue to a dance destination as we returned to North Cheam. The house lights were up, tables were being cleared away and elaborate flower arrangements, heart-shaped balloons and streamers were being shifted to new surfaces. Pink and silver seemed to be the theme for the day. Jezz's yellow shirt didn't blend in, which was a shame because it meant the guests' attention would be drawn to the reddish kebab sauce stain on our drummer's sleeve.

There were a few wedding guests at the bar at the

far end of the function room, but no one I recognised. The evening guests hadn't begun to arrive in earnest yet.

'The bar it is then,' Jezz concluded. Rather than joining the wedding guests at the function room's bar, we opted for the members' bar. Sue and I behaved ourselves and stuck to the soft drinks. Needless to say, Jezz was on the JD and Dad the Scotch.

Dad had just got the third round in when my phone buzzed. 'Where the hell are you? Boring Bren's boring and this place needs livening up.' I had just read Graham's text when Bren's best man came in and gave us the nod. We were on in fifteen minutes.

Instead of cramming another water down my throat, I opted to pay a pre-emptive visit to the men's room.

Toilet etiquette requires that, when you're having a pee, you pay as little attention as possible to the man standing at the trough adjacent to you. As a strict follower of this rule, I was surprised when the man urinating next to me started speaking.

'Wow, I can see now why she might have left you for me.'

I turned to study the speaker. Although he had dispensed with his cardigan in favour of a dark grey suit and accompanying lary pink tie, he hadn't shaved off his beard.

'Twat. How's your nose?' I asked the book dork.

'It isn't the done thing to inflict violence on some-one just because you're too thick to compete in a pub quiz, you know.'

'It isn't the done thing to sleep with someone else's wife, either.'

The dork didn't deign to respond. Instead, he turned his back on me and headed for the door.

'You didn't wash your hands,' I yelled down the corridor after him, earning the bride's brother a few disgusted glances from members of Bren's family as they were coming back from a quick fag break. Even though I got the last word in, it felt as though the dork had got the better of me on that occasion.

The night was still young, though.

Chapter Thirty-three

Lou looked stunning. Obviously the bride looked gorgeous too in her ivory meringue and her fancy, sparkly, perfectly practised hairpiece, but it was Lou who caught my eye first. She was dressed in a little black number I was convinced I had seen before. I definitely recognised her diamond necklace. It had cost me a whole month's salary on our first wedding anniversary.

Talking to the dork, Lou wasn't facing in my direction. The dork was though. When he saw me looking, he smirked at me and put his arm around my wife. My cheeks were heating up. There was no point in torturing myself so I looked away. I had a job to do after all.

Dad headed straight for the bar, as did Sue and Vee, although they did their best to put some distance between themselves and Dad. The three original members of Life in the Faz Lane took their places and waited for 'Sweet Caroline' to finish.

'You've got to love a bit of Neil Diamond. Let's hope you aren't listening to "Love on the Rocks" in the near future,' the DJ said as he handed over to us. I have heard better lines at a wedding, but at least the pancake turner had managed to get the guests up dancing.

We launched straight in with 'Marry You', which was Bren and Chelsea's eventual choice of first dance. Bren would have been much happier playing the bass than dancing. By the second verse, he was sweating profusely and gesturing frantically for family and friends to spare him his embarrassment. Graham and Amy were on their feet. More surprisingly, Dad persuaded Sue to join him. Lou was still in animated conversation with the dork.

Determined to keep as many people on the dance floor as possible, we blasted out a few of our 80s favourites. 'Let's Dance' was a big hit with the wedding crowd, the bulk of whom were our age or older. Simple Minds' 'Don't You Forget About Me' went down a treat too. We lost a few of the wrinklies, Dad and Sue included, when we moved on to 5 Seconds of Summer, but that couldn't be helped as Bren wanted modern. The grannies were probably knackered anyway.

Lou wasn't at the bar anymore. I couldn't see her or the dork anywhere. I tried to push that thought to the back of my mind as we moved back into the 80s. Duran Duran and Spandau Ballet kept people grooving until we broke for the buffet. With the whole reception singing 'Gold', I felt like a real pop star for a minute or two.

'We were fucking awesome,' Jay enthused as the two of us queued up at the buffet with the guests. Bugger my diaphragm, I was hungry.

'Mind your language, young man,' a pink and silver granny cautioned Jay.

'Sorry, Mabel. Meals on Wheels on strike next week, are they?' he asked, in reference to the pile of food clinging precariously to the old dear's plate.

'Thank God that racket has stopped,' I heard her say to her friend as she walked off in search of a chair. 'I couldn't hear myself think.'

Lou had reappeared and was talking to Sue. The two of them hadn't met before. I joined them, intrigued to know what my wife was saying to my mother.

'What woman wouldn't want to be with a man like him? He's kind, thoughtful, intelligent, reliable...' Guessing Lou wasn't talking about me, I zoned out of their conversation.

Looking around, Graham was with Amy, Jezz was with Vee, Boring Bren was with Chelsea. Even Dad and Sue seemed to be rediscovering their old spark when Sue wasn't talking to Lou. I was feeling a bit like a spare part at a wedding.

If in doubt, go to the bar. Jay was getting a swift pint in. At my request, he doubled his order.

'Why don't you do something about it if you still like her?' my cousin asked as he passed me my pint.

'Is it that obvious?'

''Fraid so. You're normally straight in there when it comes to women. What's stopping you with Lou?'

'I've tried the straight-in-there approach. I've tried the treat-'em-mean approach. Nothing seems to be working.'

'You've tried sleeping with a mate's ex, so you can tick making Lou jealous off your list of failed approaches too.'

As I was thanking Jay for his helpful observations, the pink and silver mother of the bride approached us. She even had a pink face and silver-grey hair to go with her outfit. 'Aren't you two Brendon's friends?'

'Brendon? Ah, you mean Bor…Bren,' Jay stuttered.

'Yes, we are,' I made the introductions.

'Well, you make sure he looks after my daughter. Between you and me, I don't know what she sees in him.'

'Between you and me, he's got a big cock,' Jay replied.

'I beg your pardon?'

'What woman wouldn't want to be with a man like him?' I jumped in. 'He's kind, thoughtful, intelligent, reliable. Apparently women like that sort of thing.'

'That's as maybe, but he isn't exactly a fine specimen of a man, is he? Look at how well my Geoffrey has done. He's managed to grab himself a rather attractive young filly.'

'Yeah, hasn't he done well,' I said as I turned my back on the old hag. Luckily, before we could get ourselves into any more trouble, Jezz came and dragged us back towards the stage.

Giving people a few minutes to let their Scotch eggs and quiche go down before we got too wild, we started slowly, with 'Piano Man'. Dad and Sue were the first people onto the dance floor, closely followed by the bride and Lou. The dork was talking to his dad at the bar.

More people joined the throng as we unleashed our best Monkees and Springsteen impressions. Sue and Dad did John Travolta and Olivia Newton-John proud, and before we knew it, we had come to our last song, the song that Bren and Chelsea would make their exit to.

I don't talk much during gigs, especially after offering people free beer at the end of our Raynes

Park station escapade. People haven't come to hear my wit and repartee. But on this occasion I made an exception.

'Before we get to our last song, I want to thank you for being such a great audience. Playing at a wedding is a privilege. We're being invited to share someone's special day. Chelsea and Brendon, we have loved every bit of this evening, and if we've featured positively in a few lasting memories from tonight, then we've done our job and we'll go home happy.'

And, with that, we launched into our finest Bangles impression. Sue and Vee joined us on stage as we sang 'Eternal Flame'. Chelsea dragged Bren onto the dance floor. Very quickly, either in fear of having to dance again or in anticipation of the night of passion that lay ahead of him, Bren danced Chelsea out of the social club and into the waiting wedding car.

'That's a job well done,' Jay said as the wedding guests returned to their seats to finish up their drinks or to gather their belongings together. A few of the more hardy drinkers, Jezz and Dad included, headed to the bar to get their last orders in.

The dork was holding Lou's hand and heading for the door. I hadn't got to talk to her all night, to look into her eyes, to hear her laugh. Again, Jay saw me looking. 'Don't just stand there, Dave,' he said.

He was right. I needed to stop being so wet. Without thinking, I grabbed the microphone. Desperate times called for desperate measures.

'It's hard to describe love,' I began, tentatively speaking into the microphone, 'but when it finds you, it's like an electric charge. Love makes you walk taller, run faster, dream bigger.' Some guests were giving me funny looks. Others, including Lou and the dork, didn't seem to notice my heartfelt speech. They were either too pissed to care or too preoccupied with getting the first taxi home to bed. Together.

I carried on regardless, even grew into my role. My voice got stronger as I tried to make Lou notice me. 'Love is singing at the top of your voice in the shower and not caring who hears. It's buying diamond necklaces you can't afford because you want to see that look on your lover's face when you place it around her neck. It's spending the whole night staring at you in that black dress. Anyone who thinks you look frumpy wants their eyes testing, by the way.'

'Go home, you tosser, the wedding's over,' a younger pink and silver man called from the bar.

'Love is watching some girl called Tilly run around in a corset when the football's on the other side. It's going to an art gallery when all you really want's a beer. Love gets you up in the morning, it's with you throughout the day. It takes you to bed each night. It's always by your side.'

Jezz, the man who had proposed to his girlfriend while she was washing her bits in the bath, was sticking his fingers down his throat in protest at my antics. When Vee punched him in the stomach he almost swallowed three of them. Graham too had his head in his hands. Sue and Dad, also at the bar, had slightly concerned looks on their faces. Had their son finally lost it? Probably.

'What I'm trying to say,' I continued, 'is you've got to treasure love. Look after it. I know all these things because I'm in love. I'm in love with the joint most beautiful person at this wedding tonight.'

The dork had led Lou out of the door, but was there a reluctance to leave on her part? She hadn't looked at me as she left, but she was trailing in his wake. Something told me not to give up, so I didn't.

'Louise Fazackerley, we might not exactly be love's young dream, but you know we're right together. I can be a prat. OK, I am a prat. But I'm your prat. We're meant to be together. Come back to me, Louise. Love is all around us.' And with that, I started playing.

Jay was standing by my side. He grabbed his guitar and was with me by the end of the intro. Sue and Vee were both wiping their eyes. Jezz shook his head but walked back to his drums.

Compared to spilling your heart in front of a bunch of strangers, singing is easy. You are playing a part. It isn't you. As I relaxed into the song, I looked around the now fairly empty venue.

Bren's parents and family members were sitting finishing their drinks and broadly looked to be enjoying the bonus track. The dork's mother and father, who had been putting their pink and silver coats on, were staring open-mouthed at me. Any chance of the band getting a tip had just gone out of the window.

We had only practised the Wet Wet Wet song once or twice before Christmas, when we had thought it might be the bride and groom's choice of first dance. Marti Pellow wouldn't have been too impressed, but it wasn't him I was trying to win over.

Well into the song, there was still no sign of Lou. I began to give up hope. The words weren't hitting their target so what was the point in singing them? Jay carried on strumming, but it was all beginning to die a painful death.

The coloured spots went off, replaced by the white of the fluorescent house lights. Closing my eyes and resting my head on my keyboard, I began to see images of a life without Lou. A life without colour.

And that's when I heard her voice. 'Dave Fazackerley, look at me.' She was running across the dance floor holding one high-heeled shoe in each hand. The dork was closing in fast behind her.

I opened my eyes and watched as the dork grabbed her hand. Lou turned and swung her free hand at him, her shoe connecting with his shoulder. In return the dork raised his hand.

And that's when it all kicked off. Vee, who had seen them coming before me, tried to step between Lou and the dork. The dork pushed Vee aside, thereby giving Jezz all the encouragement he needed to enter the fray. My new best mate, my boss at the bank and the drummer in my band, punched the dork for the second time in a matter of months. His punch wasn't particularly effective, more Frank Spencer than Frank Bruno, but it still managed to stop the dork in his tracks.

'That'll teach you to push my girlfriend,' Ray Winstone, no, Jezz, said as he massaged his sore knuckles.

As the dork wiped his nose on his pink sleeve, his mum pushed her husband up to defend their offspring. 'Lionel, do something.'

No wedding's complete without a good barney. 'This could get messy, Lionel,' my dad said with a manic grin on his face as the two old fogies squared up to each other. Sue stepped in and held the dads apart, sparing everyone the spectacle of a drunken geriatric tear-up.

Even the hangers-on were getting involved. A pink and silver thug had Graham in a headlock until Jay threatened to hit him with his two-thousand-pound guitar. He'd have never followed his threat through. Vee was hanging from the dork's neck in an attempt to stop him getting to Jezz. Only Amy was maintaining her dignity and not getting involved in the ruckus.

With the handbags still going on behind her, Lou looked at me. 'Aren't you going to ask me if I want to come back to yours for a coffee?'

'I thought you weren't a coffee fan?'

'I'm not, but it's what people say, isn't it?'

I took Lou's hand as she led the way towards the door.

Acknowledgements

There are a few people I would like to thank for helping me turn what was once only a vague idea into the award-winning book that it has become (OK, I might be being optimistic there, but being an author is all about self-belief).

Firstly, I would like to express my gratitude to the inventors of the Xbox for keeping my two teenage boys, Joe and William, royally entertained over the last few months while I have been working on *Six Lies*. Boys, don't worry, there'll be another book on the go soon so me demanding to spend quality time with you will only be a short-lived phenomenon.

Sue Curtis in New Zealand, you have helped me with some useful information on your home town, Palmerston North. One day, when I am up there with the likes of JK Rowling, Nick Hornby and David Nicholls, I might get to travel to exotic destinations to do my own research. Until then, I will continue to rely on friends like you.

Thank you too to the many other friends who have helped me in different ways. To Amanda, who bought copies of my first book and gave them to all her friends, to Tracey for giving me the self-belief to take the plunge as a full-time author, to Pete for making my band references authentic and to Bryn for keeping me sane when I have needed a rant. Bryn, any similarity between you and Boring Bren is totally accidental…

Finally, I would like to thank my editor, Hilary, and Helen and everyone at SilverWood Books for transforming my badly laid-out Word document into a professionally produced grown-up book, of which I am very proud.

For more information about the author and his work visit his website: www.benadamsauthor.com and follow him on Twitter @benadamsauthor

Lightning Source UK Ltd
Milton Keynes UK
UKOW04f0408301015

261726UK00002B/15/P

9 781781 32455